RUNNING HOT

Dear Editor - Book Four

EMILY SHARPE

Published by Blushing Books
An Imprint of
ABCD Graphics and Design, Inc.
A Virginia Corporation
977 Seminole Trail #233
Charlottesville, VA 22901

Emily Sharpe
Running Hot

eBook ISBN: 978-1-64563-755-4
Print ISBN: 978-1-64563-756-1
Audio ISBN: 978-1-64563-757-8
v1

Dedicated to the fine writers of Use Your Words writing group, at the Inner Truth Project in Port St. Lucie, Florida.
To fiercely brave women everywhere.
With deep gratitude for Anna Kristell and the entire team of talented, affirming folks at Blushing Books.

Author's Note

This is a work of fiction. Names, characters, businesses, events, and incidents are the products of the author's imagination. A few locations in *Running Hot* are real; others are made up. Resemblance to actual persons or events is purely coincidental, but the author sincerely hopes that all of us find the kind of love and happiness that is possible. *It's never too late!*

Summer Adventure

Despite her pregnancy, Jessica Vincent had enjoyed the road trip until today. She and her best friend, former maid of honor, and talented co-worker Donna Brown were driving to Florida with a dual purpose. They were taking Jessica's niece to Disney World but also meeting up with Donna's husband Eric, who was in Florida doing a custom stonework job. So far, the drive had been relatively trouble-free. Little Angela was precocious, but as long as she had snacks, videos to watch on her tablet, and regular potty breaks, she was an easy traveler.

For their part, Jessica and Donna always loved having time to talk about their marriages, about Jessica's pregnancy, and about their jobs at *Our City* magazine. The latest news on that front was exciting. A trial run for the national market was in the works. Jessica's husband Worth, the magazine's editor, had asked them to be on the lookout for unique, slice-of-life material as they traveled through several states.

The women chatted, sang along with the radio and kept Angela entertained as the SUV ate up the miles of highway. Six lanes had turned into four, then two. Today, they twisted and turned along the mountain road leading to Poplar Gap, a small mountain community in North Carolina.

They wondered who might get the assignments for the national debut. Although two of the magazine's top writers, neither wanted to go on the road for work. "Do you think we'll ever get to the point where we've been married for so long, time apart isn't a bad thing? I hear people talking about *wanting* more space from their spouses," Donna asked. "I can't relate."

Jessica agreed. "I miss Worth so much, it hurts. Don't get me wrong—I'm having fun, but I know my attitude is less than stellar."

More to the point, Jessica's *car's* attitude was less than stellar. At their last stop, the engine hadn't sounded right when she turned the key. The good news was that the SUV Worth had given her for Christmas was now fairly near where she planned to stop for a few hours. The plan was to visit friends in Poplar Gap for a few hours on their way to Disney World. Depending on how things were going, they might be spending the night in Georgia or north Florida.

Their friend Kristina Edwards and her beloved Ian Cameron were planning a summer wedding. From all accounts, the couple was doing well, living together on Cameron Mountain outside of Poplar Gap. Kristina's sister Layla was Jessica's sister-in-law. Layla gave Jessica strict orders to take photos of the cabin where they lived and do a bit of reconnaissance. Was Ian *really* as wonderful as Kristina seemed to think he was? Thus far, they only had the *Reader's Digest* version. Half-Cherokee, his grandfather Will Cameron had raised him. He was, according to Kristina, devastatingly handsome. They fell in love during a record-breaking, early snow just months earlier.

Layla wanted more information before she gave her blessing.

Possibly for the twentieth time in the last ten minutes, little

Angela announced from her car seat in the back that she was hungry and needed to pee. Layla's daughter had never been to Disney and was probably too young to appreciate it, but it had taken all of two seconds for Layla and her husband Keith to accept Jessica's offer. Parenthood was an energy sapper, not to mention libido. The trip would coincide with Keith's spring break from school, so they planned a stay-cation/second honeymoon. (After Jessica's call, Keith had reportedly exclaimed, "Do you think we still know how?")

Jessica caught Angela's eye in the rearview mirror. Not yet two years old, she was precocious. "Hold on, pumpkin. Aunt Donna will find you a snack, but there's no bathroom in sight, I'm afraid."

Donna rummaged in the compact cooler at her feet. She held up an apple for Jessica's approval, then handed it back to Angela. Jessica was grateful for Donna's company. Her due date wasn't until June, but her pregnant bladder required frequent pit stops, and keeping up with Angela would certainly have been more difficult without Donna along.

"How far are we from Poplar Gap?" Donna asked. They would visit Kristina and Ian for a few hours before heading south. Disney wasn't Donna's main motivation, however. Eric had been in Orlando for two months. Two *long* months. During his first trip without her, just days after their wedding, Donna had spiced things up with sexy costumes and FaceTime calls. She'd been doing the same this go 'round, but it was a poor substitute for actual skin time.

Donna continued with a sigh. "I want to check out Ian, too, but I can hardly wait to see Eric again."

Jessica laughed softly as the SUV maneuvered the winding mountain road. "I'm sure he feels the same way."

At one time, Eric had been *Jessica's* boyfriend. They had never been on the same page when it came to their emotions. Or communication. Or sexuality. Unbidden, a visual of Donna tied up in one of the couple's "red room" contraptions leapt to Jessica's mind. She shook herself to shift focus. *To each his own!* She smiled, remembering when she'd asked Worth if he had inclinations in that direction, willing to branch out depending on his response. He had assured her that their particular brand of lovemaking was exactly to his liking. *And to mine.* Just the thought of him inside of her caused her to shift in her seat. *Focus, woman.*

Jessica checked the GPS image on the phone mounted on the dashboard. "Cameron Mountain isn't far as the crow flies, but on these twisting roads, it looks like we're almost an hour away." Despite wishing to stay cheerful, the words caught in her throat. *Why in the world am I doing this? We could've flown. I miss Worth.*

"Aunt Jess. Peeeeeee. Hurry."

Jessica sighed. They would just have to wing it. It's not like anyone would see them if they stepped into the woods; there had been no traffic on the road for miles. Jessica slowed the car to a stop on the narrow shoulder and cut the engine off. "My turn for potty police," she murmured. When she got the child out of her car seat, she led her across the road behind a tree. Diapers would be easier, she thought, but leave it to Angela to do everything sooner than usual.

Angela balked a little at the thought of peeing in the woods, but necessity did indeed prove to be the mother of invention. She followed her aunt's instructions about foot placement and squatting, and soon grinned with relief. "Pee too? You pee too, Aunt Jess?"

She needed to—she *always* needed to these days—but feeling less adventurous than her niece, she opted to wait for civilization if at all possible. "I'm good," Jessica said in lilting tones. "We'll be at Aunt Kris's soon. Are you excited? *I* am. I'm excited about seeing her cabin. Excited about seeing her boyfriend. Excited about seeing Mickey Mouse." *Excited about never taking another road trip again in my life.*

Back at the car, Donna had taken the driver's seat to give Jessica a break. With Angela buckled in safely, the two women sighed in unison, anticipating a pleasant visit in their near future with clean bathrooms and adult conversation. Maybe even, in Donna's case, an adult beverage.

Donna turned the key. The engine clicked a few times but did not turn over. Jessica frowned. "Try it again."

Click-click-click. Silence. Frantically, Jessica opened the glove compartment and pulled out the paperwork stored there. The SUV was practically new. *This shouldn't be happening!* "I have no idea," Jessica said quietly. A sign ahead indicated they were approaching the town of Humphrey, population 2000. "Maybe there's a car repair shop, but how will we *get* there?" She seriously doubted there was a local branch of Triple-A. If she called her insurance company, Lord only knew how long it would take for someone to find them. *Getting away from it all is seriously overrated.*

In the side mirror, Donna saw a truck approaching and alerted Jessica.

"I hope it's someone friendly," Jessica said, turning to look. A city girl, she felt completely out of her element on a winding rural road. Trouble with a stranger was exactly what they *didn't* need.

A black man about the age of her stepfather parked behind the SUV and got out of the truck, accompanied by a beautiful but fierce looking dog. *His truck looks pretty new, anyway.* Jessica decided to meet the challenge head on. She murmured, "Maybe this fellow can help," adding, "but lock the doors just in case."

"Howdy." The man stepped closer with a warm grin but politely kept a discreet distance. The dog stuck to his side like glue, evidently well-trained. "What seems to be the problem?"

Jessica threw up her hands in exasperation. "I have no idea! The engine was slow to start earlier today, and now it won't start at all. We've been on the road several days, with a toddler." She pointed to the back seat, where Angela happily munched her apple. *Might as well lay the "damsels in distress" on thick.* She pointed to her stomach. "And I'm pregnant."

"So I see! Congratulations. So where're you headed?" The man walked around the car slowly, looking for obvious issues, stopping to wave cheerfully and smile at Donna and the child. Now and then, he'd reach down and scratch the dog's short gray coat as if to reassure him that all was well.

Maybe it wasn't the wisest thing to do, laying all her proverbial cards on the table with a stranger, but as a journalist, Jessica also trusted her instincts. She'd bet money this man was one of the good guys. "Eventually, we're aiming for Disney World, but today, we're expected in Poplar Gap."

The man grinned even wider. "Do tell! That's my stomping ground."

"Do you know Kristina Edwards and Ian Cameron?"

The man laughed and held out his hand. "I sure do! Name's Chip Murphy, ma'am. Ian's my nephew, as a matter of fact. Tina was my neighbor before she moved in with him."

Jessica was so relieved, she trotted closer and threw her arms around Chip. "Chip, of course! I'm Kristina's sister's sister-in-law. Shirttail relative, but I've heard a slew of stories about you!"

Chip held Jessica at arm's length and rolled his eyes, chuckling. "I'll just bet you have." The previous October, Chip had helped Ian's grandfather with his cockamamie plan to find a suitable woman for Ian. Kristina had virtually been kidnapped. When an unseasonably heavy snow trapped her in the cabin with Ian alone—and trapped the others down the mountain— Kristina and Ian had promptly fallen in love. It had been quite the winter, filled with new and renewed relationships.

"So you're Will and Eleanor's long-lost son. We've heard so much about you and your parents, too. How are they? I'd love to meet them." She whipped her head around and shot Donna a *you're-not-going-to-believe-this* look. Will and Eleanor, a local black girl, had been in love as teenagers, but her parents had whisked her away before Will even knew she was pregnant with his child. Worth had been instrumental in researching Chip's adoption papers, as well as helping Kristina resolve something from her past. *This may be just the kind of story Worth is looking for.*

Chip became serious. "I'm forever grateful to your husband, ma'am. *Darn* it. My folks are away for a week or so, visiting friends in Asheville. I drove them over just this morning." He rubbed his chin in thought. "It's probably the battery. I can give you a jump-start, or I can tow you to Pete Cummings' shop, then drive you to the cabin. Depending on what's wrong with the car, you might have a bit of a stay, but I'll bet the young'un will love it."

"It's not the battery," Jessica said. "I don't know much about cars, but I know that much. This is a new car. Can't be the battery." She sighed. "We need to know that it's fixed before we head south. Tow, please!"

Jessica stood and watched as Chip expertly pulled his truck in front of her SUV. When he let the tailgate down to pull off the heavy tow chain stored there, his dog jumped into the bed of the truck. Chip slammed the tailgate back in place. "Blue wants to be my look-out, apparently. We'll take it nice and slow, Blue," Chip said, then he turned to Jessica. "Just keep the wheel steady."

"Is Mr. Cummings, um, reasonable?" Jessica asked.

Chip laughed. "Doesn't really matter, does it? Come to think of it, I heard he's been under the weather, but don't worry. Andy'll take good care of you. Now put 'er in neutral and make sure the brake's off. Get set for a little yank when we get started. I'll go slow."

Soon the two vehicles were back on the road. Jessica didn't take her eyes off Chip's bumper while Donna tried not to notice the occasional sharp drop-offs. She chattered breezily to Angela, pointing out wildflowers and trees to keep both their minds occupied. Even going at a snail's pace, it wasn't long before Chip pulled into a service station on the edge of town bearing a bright sign that announced, "Pete's Place."

"Mountain?" Angela chirped.

Jessica giggled. "One of them, sweetheart. Not Aunt Kristina's yet, but we'll be there soon. Hopefully." She stretched from the pent-up tension on the road and opened first, her door, then Angela's, as Donna got out and breathed in the mountain air.

Jessica frowned at Blue. "Is he, um, staying back there?"

In answer, Chip lowered the tailgate. The dog took off like a shot into the woods behind the service station. "Blue wouldn't hurt a soul unless I told him to," he said, "but he'd just as soon play while we're here."

Satisfied that it was a safe environment for a child, Jessica unbuckled the straps on Angela's car seat. "Up you go, baby!" she said brightly.

Angela frowned as her tiny feet hit the ground. "Not baby. *You* baby," she said authoritatively, patting Jessica's stomach. Angela looked around and suddenly squealed with delight. "Unca Worth!" she cried, running in the direction of the garage.

Jessica's eyes followed Angela. Of course, it wasn't Worth. Worth was at home, working in his office at the magazine. In the semi-darkness of the garage's interior, she could definitely see why Angela had been confused, however. A figure in overalls, shorter than Worth but not by much, faced away from them. Under a baseball cap, a bald head was visible that looked, for all the world, like Worth's. Even though her brain told her it was impossible that he'd be working on cars in North

Carolina, the familiar sight of a bald head made Jessica's heart leap.

Chip saw her staring inside the garage. "There's Andy right there," he said as he unhooked the chain and threw it back into the bed of his truck.

Angela pulled on the leg of the overalls. When Andy turned around, Jessica's jaw dropped. Andy's face was unmistakably female.

The twenty-something young woman took off her baseball cap to wipe perspiration away with a fairly clean cloth from her bib pocket and adopted a stern expression. "Does this little girl belong to anyone, or do I have to keep her?"

Angela giggled. "Funny head. Can't keep me. I with them." She pointed at Jessica. "Aunt Jess, Aunt Donna. Taking to Mickey Mouse. That brown man helped. Big dog."

Before Jessica could die of embarrassment, Chip nodded. "You know your colors, little lady. I am indeed brown." He bent over to compare his strong arm with Angela's tiny pale one. "Mine's a lot browner than yours, but if you're headed to Florida, that could change."

Angela giggled again. Used to being the center of attention at home, she loved every second of it now. Suddenly, she frowned at Andy. "Why no hair?"

Before Andy could answer, a young man about her age pulled into the station on a five-speed bicycle. His long dark hair was pulled back into a ponytail under the bike helmet, which he removed and hung by its strap on the handlebars. He waved but said nothing.

"Hey, Jeffrey. Jeffrey Wilson, meet..." Andy's voice drifted off. "...a smart little girl and her friends. They just got here, thanks to Mr. Murphy." She addressed Jessica and Donna. "Chip brings stranded drivers here fairly regularly."

"You can pay me with a cold drink," Chip teased, "before they hear about the really *good* shop down the road."

Jessica held out a hand to Andy. "Jessica Vincent. And this is Donna Brown. The small talkative person is my niece. Chip says you work wonders."

While Jeffrey watched and listened, Andy asked detailed questions about any sounds or smells Jessica had noticed and the car's service record. "It's probably the battery," Andy said.

"It's not the battery!" Jessica insisted. "I'm sure of that much, anyway. The car's brand new, almost. But we've got so far to go, I want to make sure it's safe before we head out. How will we get it into the garage?"

Jeffrey had stood a little stiffly off to one side, but now he stepped closer. "I'll help," he said. "Someone should get in the car and steer while I push with you and Chip." When Jessica turned and he saw her pregnant profile, his eyebrows shot up.

Jessica laughed. "How about *I* get in the car and steer while the rest of *you* push?"

Soon the SUV was high above their heads on the hydraulic lift. Andy frowned as she walked underneath the chassis. "I'll check everything out, of course, but my money's still on the battery. Don't worry, though. Whatever's fucked up, I'll fix it."

Surprised by both the bald head and bad language, Donna asked casually, "How long are we talking about?" Every delay put her that much further from reuniting with Eric.

Andy did some mental calculations, making little grimaces as she did so. "As late as it's getting, you should plan on tomorrow."

Jessica caught the disappointment in Donna's eyes and shrugged. "We're driving to Florida. Since we'll be in Orlando several days, maybe a patch job now, as long as it's safe? Then I could get it repaired properly there?"

Andy nodded. "I'll make some calls, see if I can't recommend someone there." She looked away to mutter, "It's the battery."

When Chip whistled, Blue bounded through the trees and

jumped up onto the bed of the truck. "Let's get you up to Cameron Mountain," he said, slamming the tailgate closed. "Can you bring the car down again, Andy? We'll need that car seat and their bags. It's gonna be a little tight but at least I've got the double cab now. If I still had my old truck, we'd have to stick the little one in back."

Angela jumped up and down. "Ride in back with Blue! Pleaaaaaase?"

Jeffrey was horrified. "Oh, *no*, Mr. Murphy! That would be against the law. It wouldn't be safe. I'm surprised you would even—"

Chip slapped the young man playfully on the shoulder. "I'm kidding! Principal Clark would have my hide if I put young'uns in the back. You know that! Jeffrey here's a senior at Humphrey K-12, where my lady friend is the principal. Kristina works there, too."

"Miss Edwards is my teacher," Jeffrey smiled proudly. "She's the best."

Well, that explains a lot, thought Jessica. There was something about Jeffrey she hadn't been able to put her finger on, but now she understood. Kristina worked with autistic students in the school's Exceptional Education and Student Services department. Jeffrey must be one of her high functioning students. Jessica smiled warmly at the young man. "A senior! Congratulations! What are your plans after that, do you know?"

Andy leaned her shoulder in against Jeffrey's. From a distance, Jessica thought they would look like buddies, maybe brothers.

"Jeffrey and I went to school together *forever*," Andy said. "When he graduates, he wants to stick around and help with ESE, don't you, Jeffrey? He's great with younger kids."

"Are you going to be a senior too, then?" Donna asked in a tone that Jessica recognized as the journalist in her digging for details. Andy looked older than high school, but then, so did Jeffrey. Maybe it was her extreme hairstyle.

Andy lowered her voice while Jeffrey took Angela by the hand through the shop's little waiting room into the adjoining store for a snack. "I'm twenty-two. I graduated five years ago. Jeffrey's twenty, but he's been a senior a while. His mother wasn't sure he was ready to leave school yet. Jeffrey says that's pretty common with parents of autistic kids." She smiled suddenly. "Jeffrey's a fucking genius, though, in his own way."

Her smile, even on a dirty face, was dazzling, transforming her from boyish to beautiful. Donna and Jessica were dying to ask about her baldness. Her enormous hazel eyes and eyebrows suggested that her hair, if she'd had any, would be dark brown.

Andy caught them staring and sobered quickly. "Jeffrey's mother just went through her final round of chemo," she explained. "Fucking cancer. Jeffrey didn't want her to feel alone when her hair started falling out, but he has this, um, *thing* about his own hair. He can't stand to have anybody touch it." She gave a little shrug and looked past them into the bright sunlight. "I said I'd do it instead." She rubbed her head. "It'll grow back."

Angela ran up, clutching a bag of chips. "You gotta see, Aunt Jess. Pretty!" Grabbing Jessica by the hand, she pulled her with all the strength in her little arms, with Donna following. Inside the small waiting area, was an exquisite mural portraying, they assumed, the history of the town. The faces were portrayed in such detail, they looked ready to speak at any moment.

Jeffrey beamed at their oohs and ahhs. "I took photographs and printed them on cards, if you'd like to see them."

Jessica smiled. "What a smart thing to do! This art work is far too good to just stay on a wall."

Jeffrey led her to the rack inside the store where colorful cards and matted prints were neatly wrapped in clear plastic.

Jessica took one of each from the rack and turned them over. "Who's the artist? I don't see a name anywhere."

Jeffrey nodded his head toward the garage. "Andy. Andy is the artist."

Jessica's eyes narrowed in thought as she flipped through the artwork. *An artist who doesn't sign her art, who works in a car shop, and who shaved her head in solidarity with a cancer patient, who may have one of the prettiest smiles I've seen, and who cusses like a longshoreman. If that's not a human interest story people would love, I don't know what is.*

2

Andy

Just as Andy had predicted, the problem on Jessica's car was the battery. She called the nearest auto parts supplier and was promised delivery by nine the next morning. As Jeffrey kept her company, she went over every nook and cranny of the SUV, making sure everything else was shipshape.

Driving to Jeffrey's house on the other side of town, with his bike in the back of Andy's light truck, they listened to their favorite station on the radio, singing along. Andy had a good ear, better than Jeffrey's, but he remembered the lyrics more precisely.

During a commercial, Andy turned the volume down to ask about his mother. Her last treatment had been two months before and she was feeling much better. She still wore colorful scarves and the occasional wig in public, but her oncologist had said her hair would probably start growing back in a month or so.

Jeffrey never failed to mention what he called Andy's *sacrifice*. "You are braver than I am. Stronger. I wish I..." His voice trailed off as he stared out the open window of the truck.

Andy reached over to squeeze her friend's hand. "I did it for you, not for your mom. But she's the fucking rock star, Jeffrey. *She's* the one who's brave and strong, raising you alone all this time, then cancer." She'd always admired Marilda Wilson. Her husband had left town soon after Jeffrey was diagnosed as a toddler, unable to accept the fact that autism wasn't something he could fix. When her own mother had left, Mama Wilson, as she called her, had been a welcoming surrogate.

"Rock star, rock star, *movie* star," Jeffrey mused. There was an actor from his mother's childhood she had told him about. A Star Wars movie. No, Star *Trek*. With a bald woman. "A beautiful bald woman," Jeffrey exclaimed, snapping his fingers. "Persis Khambatta."

Jeffrey rattled off all the statistics and dates about the woman. He loved facts and figures, memorizing them instantly. "Mama said you are prettier than she was. I looked her up. Persis Khambatta was prettier, but she died in 1998. So now you are prettier."

It was late. Andrea Elizabeth Cummings sat at the vanity mirror in her room inspecting her hands. However hard she scrubbed them, stubborn grease usually lurked beneath a fingernail or two; tonight was no exception.

Andy looked at her reflection now in the mirror, smiling at the memory of Jeffrey's words. Jeffrey always told the truth. She turned her head this way and that. According to her father's photo album, she favored her mother, a wild child who had grown weary of her father, the mountains, and her children, though not necessarily in that order. Andy had vague memories of a pretty woman with long hair who had smiled across the kitchen table from her high chair, but that was it. As soon as her mother had gotten the chance to leave Humphrey, she'd taken it.

Andy grimaced. *How many times have I heard* that *fucking story over the years?* A broken down bus containing a traveling blue-grass band. Her father had worked on the engine while the drummer worked on her mother. She loved to sing, did she? They'd been talking about adding a female vocalist. Within a few days, she was gone. Occasionally, they'd get a postcard, which Pete would have one of the boys read at supper before shaking his head sadly and adding it to the little stack on the fireplace. Andy always got the feeling her father hoped she would return home.

After a few years, the postcards stopped. Pete Cummings raised his sons and daughter with the help of neighbors and relatives, but Andy survived the abundance of testosterone in the house by scrapping and clawing her way out of scuffles. She was fishing with them by the time she was five and changing tires when she was ten. Although Pete didn't approve, he also did not correct his children's colorful language unless there was trouble at school or church. He had enough to worry about without that.

At school, Andy had been The Girl Without a Mother. The Girl Who Didn't Like Dolls. As she got older, she was the first girl picked for teams but the last girl asked out on dates. She was the girl who got "volun-told" for art projects around town but who sat home every Saturday night.

Even the guys who admired and respected her for her many abilities, to say nothing of her outrageous cussing, assumed that the overalls and baggy shirts she preferred must cover a body that was, if not exactly *male*, not what they desired, either. Besides, weird Jeffrey and she were practically joined at the hip. In a small town like Humphrey, everyone knew them, loved them, and would have taken poorly to *outsiders* teasing them, but they were still considered "different." Set apart.

Sporting a shaved head only made it worse. She stared at the reflection, trying to be objective. Her eyes were big and expressive—a plus. She smiled, something she did not do often, satisfied with her even, white teeth. She'd always worn her hair long, from impatience, rather than vanity. Beauty parlors? No, thank you. It had been easier for her father to yank it back into a ponytail when she was little; she'd worn it like that ever since.

Jeffrey had done the honors of cutting the tail off for her on that fateful day last month, but then she'd whacked away with her scissors before shaving it herself, feeling her scalp with the free hand until every inch of its surface was as smooth as it could be. Pete had checked, grunted his approval, and muttered something about being as wild as her mother. She sighed. She loved Pete—Daddy—but it was obvious that he wasn't happy.

It seemed that everyone in her life was lonely, including herself. Even her closest friend Jeffrey was honest about facts but not his emotions. She wasn't sure if he even felt things the way she felt them. She'd learned to read him over the years in a measure: Happy Jeffrey was different from Sad or Afraid Jeffrey. But Loving Jeffrey was an enigma. He was twenty. Didn't guys want girl-friends at twenty? Sex? Her brothers had; that was for damn sure.

Oldest brother Clyde got his girlfriend pregnant when they were seventeen, moving to Asheville, where he worked on the grounds crew at Biltmore House, the famous estate of the Vanderbilts. A second baby followed the first, then a third. His wife babysat a few neighbor kids to help out, saying she didn't need a diploma because she had a family. She and Andy got along, but they had little in common. Andy wanted…well, she wasn't sure, but it was more than she had. More than what kept her sister-in-law happy.

The middle child, Chance, went into the army after high school, breaking several local hearts of various ages when he left. He planned to make the military a career, right up until his Jeep hit an IED in Kabul last year. Recovering quickly, he now kept the vehicles at Fort Bragg in tiptop condition instead of dodging the Taliban. The last time he'd called, he said he was dating a girl who worked as a bartender in Fayetteville.

Andy envisioned a string of nephews and nieces in her future but no children of her own. Pete may have dreamed of his sons taking over the shop one day, but it was Andy he depended on. That this plan narrowed his daughter's prospects for a husband, was something he tried not to think about. Andy didn't think about it, either. For a long time, she had taken it for granted that she would take care of the shop and her father, be a beloved aunt, encourage Jeffrey, and never marry. Maybe, one day, like the artist Grandma Moses, she'd begin painting seriously in her seventies and even achieve fame.

Only once had a blip appeared on her romantic screen, one man who had made her feel special. Andy pulled out a vanity drawer and took out a small velvet box. Opening the hinged lid, she fingered the gold necklace there. She took it out and ran a finger over her initials, etched fancily on the front, then turned it over. GFS. The date of the gift was just eight years earlier, but it felt like a lifetime ago. And it still made her angry.

The year Andy turned twelve, a new preacher came to Humphrey Bible Church, a small but active non-denominational congregation. Jeffrey's mother asked her to join her and Jeffrey on his first Sunday in town. She'd enjoyed the music especially. The charismatic preacher had wavy black hair, a quick wit and easy laugh, two sons close to Andy's age and a pleasant, albeit plain, wife.

Soon the whole town was enamored. The men thought highly of him while many of the women, Andy noticed, all but gushed when he was around. No one noticed Andy if she chose to fade into the background, and as this described the majority of the time, she picked up on quite a few interesting tidbits of information about the Sanderson family. George Frederick Sanderson.

Reverend Sanderson noticed her, apparently recognizing potential no one else could. Maybe it was because she was one of the few females in town who kept him at arm's length. She liked his sermons and she liked his sons. She liked his wife Sylvia. But there was something about *him* that put her off. He stood too close. His eyes looked at her with too much intensity. Something about him both attracted and repelled her. His attention confused her, but there was no one she could talk to about it. Everyone adored him.

One day, when she was thirteen, he made her mad. *What was it? Oh, yes. He fussed at Sylvia at the station in front of the boys and me. He could tell I didn't like that.* When he saw her expression, he pulled her aside. "Oh now, don't be mad. We can kiss and make up."

The remark upset her so much that she'd rehearsed a little speech. She planned to tell him off, put him in his place. But as the days dragged on, she decided he might have meant that he'd make up with Sylvia. Either that, or he was teasing. Whatever the truth, she never mentioned it. And over the next year, he made it a point to include her in family events. She should call them George and Sylvia. He made her feel special. He'd given her the necklace at Christmas, quietly explaining that if anyone asked why his initials were on the back, to tell them they stood for "Grateful For my Salvation."

One Saturday afternoon, the summer Andy was fourteen,

she was helping her father at the station when George stopped by. He pulled a picnic basket from the backseat and swung it up in the air, calling her over. "I'm taking this up to the lake to meet Sylvia and boys. Want to come with?"

Before she could answer, her father nodded. "Sure thing, Preacher. It's a slow day. You've earned a day off, Andy."

It was a beautiful day for the lake. She was used to running errands here and there with him. Still, when she slid into the front seat, she sat close to the door. George laughed, not unkindly. "You're not afraid of me, are you, Andrea?"

That was another thing. No one else had called her Andrea since her mother left. "I'm not afraid of anything," she said softly, which made him laugh again. He reached across the seat and gently took her hand, stroking it with his thumb as he drove and talked.

On the way to the lake, something inside reminded her of the red flags, the distrust, her former misgivings, but she dismissed them as ridiculous signs of her past immaturity. She mattered to this man. And she was fourteen, much older than twelve.

"You can move closer, Andrea," he said. "I would like that very much."

"Where are Sylvia and the boys?" she asked, sliding over. It wasn't unusual for her to sit close to him, she reasoned. When she went places with the family, she sat between him and Sylvia while the boys and Jeffrey filled the back seat.

"It's just you and me, Andrea," he said with a little wink. "A white lie. They're in Asheville today. I've been wanting to spend some time just with you, though, to talk some serious matters over."

Andy was almost amused. No one else treated her that way, not even Jeffrey. Strange, strong feelings washed over her, making her breathe funny. It felt good sitting close to him. When she leaned forward to turn on the radio at his request, his arm brushed her breast, hidden and protected inside her overalls from work. Andy squirmed away a bit but didn't think anything of it.

At the lake, when George pulled out a blanket from the trunk, Andy helped spread it on the grass beneath a tall poplar tree. The picnic lunch was egg salad sandwiches and potato chips, with chilled bottles of soda to wash it down. She couldn't get over the fact that this grown man didn't treat her like a child. He was so mature compared to the boys her age. He was smart, funny, and handsome. On top of that, he reminded her of the Bible characters he preached about, larger than life. In a way she didn't know how to explain, she felt closer to God when she was with him.

And now, she was so engrossed in her lunch and the sounds of dragonflies buzzing in the cattails at the shore, she didn't notice how much closer George had gotten. "Have you been reading your Bible, Andrea?" he asked softly, startling her from her reverie.

Shaking her head shyly, she was filled with regret. She had disappointed him, surely.

"There's something very special mentioned in St. Paul's writings that I want to share with you," he explained. "It's called 'the laying on of hands.' It will make you feel God's power right down to your core."

Andy put the necklace back in the drawer beneath a handkerchief that had belonged to her mother and took off her overalls. She draped them over the footboard of her four-poster bed for the next day and pulled her shirt over her head. Naked, she inspected her figure in the mirror. Unbeknownst to everyone but the town's doctor, Andy had developed early, at about age twelve. Coincidentally, about the same time the Sandersons came to town.

Andy shuddered at the memory of the lake, pulling a simple cotton nightgown over her head, another hand-me-down from her mother. George had kissed her on the blanket at the lake with lips that were softer than satin, her first kiss. He had gently stroked her cheek, her hair, her arm. She had enjoyed the kissing very much. At one point, he had moved her hand onto his arm, inviting her to touch him.

Andy crawled under her covers and closed her eyes, seeing it all again, that moment when she'd realized that he had unbuckled her overalls and pulled down the bib top, his hand moving under her shirt to discover firm, unfettered breasts. It had felt nice, this laying on of hands. She remembered thinking it was no wonder her silly friends talked about boys and kissing and everything all the time. But they couldn't know about this. This was not something children could know about. This was…holy.

Andy's overalls and shoes were off before she became frightened. She didn't know much, but she knew a preacher—or any man old enough to be her father—shouldn't be taking her clothes off. He shouldn't be pulling that *thing* out of his pants. She was horrified. Living with two brothers, she'd seen glimpses of their little drooping penises; they'd taken baths together as children. They joked about their portable toys, fumbling around in their shorts with glee, making her wonder why their bodies seemed to be more fun that hers. But *this*. It was wide as the gearshift knob in Daddy's truck, pulsing, alive, dripping with something as it stood straight in the sunshine as he knelt beside her.

She hit him on the head with her empty bottle of soda,

gathered up her overalls and flip flops quickly, and ran into the woods. She thought she might have killed him and half hoped she had, but what would people say? Would they believe her? That thing would have hurt her. She was sure of it, for all his sweet quotes from scripture. If that was what it took to feel the power of God, she'd do without, thank you.

She'd stopped running only long enough to put her clothes back on. On the pavement finally, she flagged down Chase's car when he drove past with one of his girlfriends. "What the heck are you doin' out here?"

"I'll tell you later," she said, feeling sick. "Just take me home."

That night, Andy related what had transpired. She didn't know the mechanics or all the terminology, but Pete Cummings got the picture, resolving to ask Jeffrey's mother to explain the birds and the bees properly to his daughter, regretting that he had waited this long.

Sending Andy to bed with assurances she had done nothing wrong, Pete Cummings and his two teenage sons had a come-to-Jesus moment with the Reverend Sanderson. He had two choices: leave Humphrey immediately, or they'd tell his wife and sons, then the church, then the whole town. Maybe by then, the law would have time to arrive and they would string him up by his balls. If George Sanderson underestimated Andrea Cummings' willingness to tell on him after years of careful, discreet years of grooming, he was quickly convinced.

Sunday morning, Andy went to church with the Wilsons, just like her father suggested. When the Sandersons didn't show up, people turned this way and that in their pews, sensing that something was up. Finally, the head deacon stepped into the pulpit, hemming and hawing through a vague explanation. Reverend Sanderson and the family had left town during the night. No, all the money was there. It was nothing like that. They didn't know why, maybe never would, but the pulpit committee would meet after the service to begin searching for a replacement. "In the meantime, please turn to 312 in your hymnbooks."

"Well, I swanny," Mrs. Wilson muttered. "I always thought there was something a little off about that one."

Neither Andy nor her father or brothers ever said a word.

Andy fluffed the pillow and turned over. Overalls had been practical, working in the shop, but they became her uniform after that day. She couldn't remember the last time she'd worn a dress or gone swimming in a group. The cussing became habitual. At school, she'd change into PE clothes inside a shower stall, preferring the whispered remarks about her shyness to exposing herself.

She reached up to the crown of her smooth head and let her hands follow her contours down her slender neck, melon-sized breasts, flat stomach and under the simple shift, to the little patch of curly hair between her legs. She was older now. She'd read books and magazine articles. She'd seen movies. Jeffrey's mother had educated her thoroughly and, she thought, a bit wistfully, as if the subject matter was something she missed. That in itself had been educational.

She had learned to touch herself in ways that sent shivers of pleasure throughout her. It *must* be wonderful to be with a man; it *must* be better than this. Poetry, songs, movies, even watching couples in town—everything pointed to sex being amazing. Kristina had even asked her to paint a mural at Exagorà House as a celebration of the human anatomy and sexuality. You don't celebrate something that isn't wonderful.

Andy hadn't had a clue what to paint, studying Georgia O'Keefe's vaginal blooms, looking at calla lilies, studying nudes and tattoo books. The result was, even to her own eyes, amazing. Some of the women and girls who made their way inside the building were initially shocked, but the images were also oddly comforting. They had been hurt, bruised either figuratively or physically or both, but there, inside those colorful walls, it was appropriate to celebrate their gender.

Andy wondered if one day, a man would celebrate *her*, a man who could see beyond the engine grease and overalls again. She made no excuses for George Sanderson. He had been wrong. He had stirred feelings he had no right to stir. Was she as special as he had made her feel, or was it all a lie to serve his selfish purposes?

3

The Mountain

As Andy worked on the SUV, the others enjoyed a lovely drive to Cameron Mountain and a visit on the porch. "Won't you stay for supper?" Kristina asked as Chip finally stood up from the swing. Angela played happily in the wide open area in front of the beautiful log cabin. It was clear that Blue wanted to jump in with her but obediently stayed at Chip's feet.

Ian chuckled. "I think Chip's got other plans." Half Cherokee, Ian Cameron was not as dark as his half-black uncle. His skin was ruddier, like honey in the sunlight. And he was so handsome that Jessica and Donna were constantly distracted by him as they watched Angela's antics. There was something *primeval* about him. His jet-black hair fell to his shoulders, but his eyes were pale blue from genes inherited from his father.

Chip nodded. "I've got an invitation to join Ellen tonight, but thank you, Tina." Despite his friend's return to her given name, he preferred the nickname she had used the summer before. Ellen Clark was the ebony-skinned and full-figured school principal as well as Kristina's boss. Chip hoped that soon, she would be more than that to him.

Jessica drew in a breath, realizing suddenly that she'd been staring at Ian. "I promised Layla I would take lots of photos," she said, pulling her phone from her purse. "Do you mind?" She grouped everyone in several configurations on the porch and in the yard. Ian was so tall, he stood center back in each one.

"Let me hold the phone to get you in here too," he offered. "My arms are long."

I'll bet that's not all, Jessica thought. *Sorry about that, Worth! I miss you!* "Let's see. We've met Chip, Ian, Andy, Jeffrey... Wilson, is it?" When Ian smiled at her, her knees went a bit weak. *No wonder Kristina fell for this one so fast.*

Ian put an arm around Kristina's shoulder and hugged her to him as she gazed up at him. "Jeffrey's quite a guy, isn't he? He and Andy have been pals as long as I can remember. And Andy's quite the mechanic."

Chip opened his truck door to let Blue jump inside. "I can pick you up tomorrow and take you to the shop, Jessica."

"No worries, Chip," Kristina offered. "One of us'll do it. I'm so excited! I mean, I hate that you had car trouble, Jess, but now we get to have everyone a whole night instead of just a few hours. What a treat!"

As Chip's truck disappeared into the woods, the others sat back down on the porch. The sun was still bright as it lowered toward the treetops, but it was a comfortable, breezy afternoon, with just a slight nip in the air. "I can see why so many people spend their springs and summers in the mountains," Donna said. "Angela's having a blast, isn't she?"

Jessica laughed. "I'll bet she's never been this dirty in her life. Layla keeps her dolled up and prissy, but I think this is great for her."

Kristina rocked peacefully in a chair beside Ian, holding his hand. "Layla still tries to mother *me*, so I can just imagine what she's like with Angela. I guess that comes from losing your mother as young as we did. You're so blessed to have Carol, Jess." She paused. "How about you, Donna? Does your mother live close to you?"

Donna explained that her mother had had substance abuse issues, leaving her and her father when she was six and later dying of a drug overdose. She had no intention of spoiling the afternoon with the sad tale of her father's abuse, but it did bring something to mind. "I hear you started a support group for victims of sexual violence, am I right? How's that going?"

Ian beamed at his wife. "It's going well. We rented a space in Humphrey and talked a family counselor into locating there —she has her own practice, of course, but she's available to our group, too."

Jessica was intrigued. "Really! It's such a small town—I mean, not as small as Poplar Gap," she said with a chuckle, "but I'm surprised there's enough business for her to move here."

Kristina's eyes sparkled. "Oh, you'd be surprised. Helen— that's her name, Helen Hamilton—planned to retire but hated to give up counseling completely. She stays pretty busy with unhappy marriages and troubled kids, but she's been incredible with our clients. We call it Exagorà House, after the grant provider. Worth really helped us out. Helped *me* out."

Jessica nodded. "He was delighted to do so. When Layla shared what happened, just the details she knew, I hoped Worth could get to the bottom of things, provide closure. Of course, there was no way of knowing what all would result."

Kristina beamed at Ian. "When Ian's grandfather and Chip trapped me up here with this guy, Ian assured me that I had the wrong idea about what happened to me in college. I just didn't know *how* wrong until Worth brought us all together."

Kristina had been drugged at a frat party in college and raped by three students. For years, she had thought it was her fault, but Ian convinced her that she must have been drugged.

Worth tracked down the mysterious group, Exagorà Foundation, that had sent her a generous grant. When he discovered that the foundation was comprised of the rapists' fathers, he brought fathers and sons to apologize to Kristina in person. The icing on the cake? A new grant, renewable each year, for Kristina to use for her school or whatever she chose. Starting Exagorà House was one of her first actions.

"Exagorà means 'redemption,' as I recall," Jessica said. "A perfect name."

Donna frowned. "That's wonderful, Kristina. Really. I wish there had been—I mean, I never told anyone but Eric, but I was a victim. A survivor, I prefer. At the time, I didn't have anyone to tell or anywhere to turn. There are resources in the city now, of course, but how awesome to have something *here*. Abuse isn't limited to big cities."

Jessica reached out a hand to squeeze Donna's. Maybe they'd have time to talk about it on the trip to Florida. She hoped so. Donna had become such a close friend over the last few years, she was a little surprised she'd never mentioned the abuse before. Her stomach groaned, reminding her of how long it had been since they'd eaten. "Can I take us out to dinner? What is there around here?"

Ian laughed. "Francine's Diner is the only place in Poplar Gap, but I was thinking—"

"Pizza!" Angela shouted from the yard. She had stopped doing somersaults long enough to overhear the conversation on the porch. "I want pizza!"

Kristina shook her head. "I'm afraid the nearest pizza place is so far away, they don't deliver here, sweet pea."

Angela scowled and crossed her arms. "I want pizza," she said, as if her desire was all it took to conjure a meal.

Jessica raised her eyebrows at the others. "I think someone's used to getting her way at home," she said quietly. "The time away may be good for Layla and Keith *and* for Angela. For me too," she said, patting her belly. "You ignore behavior at home, but then wham! Get around new people and the spoiling's obvious. I apologize."

Ian bounced from the porch to the yard and scooped Angela up as she shrieked with delight. Holding her under an arm, he swung her around. "I thought I heard a little girl say something, but where did she go? All I hear is a little pig."

Angela giggled and squealed. Ian threw her gently onto the ground and tickled her, then made a big show of scrambling away on his hands and knees, encouraging her to climb all over him and tickle him back.

"Ian's good with kids," Donna mused, catching Jessica's eye and winking.

Kristina caught the exchange. "We definitely want a family," she agreed. "Maybe not right away, although we're not doing anything to stop it, really. And doing plenty to try!" She laughed. "I'm still amazed by it all, you know? When I met you both, I was this shy, mousy *victim*, afraid of men, afraid of strangers, even myself. And now look at us."

Kristina had met the women when she spent a Christmas vacation helping Layla with baby Angela, who had come prematurely. Briefly, it had been touch-and-go with both mother and child. Facing that dire possibility had inspired Kristina to get the help she needed. Aided by a mysterious grant, she had found a therapist who helped immensely. Wanting to start fresh in a new job and location, she'd met Ian. "I'm the luckiest woman in the world," Kristina said softly.

Ian stood and dangled Angela by a foot safely but high enough off the grass that she screamed and laughed simultaneously. "How about instead of pizza," he asked Angela, "I grill us some nice juicy burgers!"

Kristina looked at her friends and whispered. "Let's not tell her it's venison, okay? Some kids have a problem eating Bambi."

"That was delicious," Donna said as she cleared the table. "I'd heard venison was too lean for good burgers."

"The trick is to add a bit of fat and season it properly," said Kristina. "I'm learning! With just a wood stove and microwave, Ian's grill comes in handy quite often. He hunts, he cleans, he cooks."

I'll bet he does more than that, Donna thought, feeling a familiar warmth between her legs. *If I don't get to Eric soon, I may not be responsible for my actions.*

The women chatted easily as they cleaned up. When Donna mentioned the mural at the garage, Kristina enthusiastically described the one Andy had completed at Exagorà House. "We've had some folks come to our open houses who turn white as a sheet when they look closely at a gorgeous flower, only to realize it has a clitoris! I love it. Andy's talented, but she won't find much recognition in Humphrey, I'm afraid. And that mouth of hers! Maybe that's what comes from not having a mom around, I don't know. Our grandmother would've tanned our hides if we talked like that."

Donna glanced out the front window, to see Ian and Angela chasing fireflies in the cool mountain air. Jessica stood under the first stars of the evening, talking on her phone. If they had to be delayed, she decided this was an excellent place to be. "I've never experienced the quiet of a mountain, so different than quiet of the city at night or even the beach. The trees seem to capture every sound," she said.

"You should be here in the winter," Kristina said with a smile. "Last winter, when we had that huge snow, it was like being inside a cotton ball, it was so quiet. Walking outside was like being in church when everyone lowers their voices." She bent down to put away a serving dish, then grew serious as she stood. "You mentioned being a survivor. Is it something you'd like to talk about?"

Donna shrugged. "One day. It was all so long ago. Talking it over with Eric helped a lot. At first, he weirded out on me, making assumptions, thinking only about what it might mean to *him*, but when we really talked about it, it was all good."

Kristina gave Donna a warm hug. "My therapist out west, Elizabeth, did wonders, but Ian is the one who pulled me out of the mire. He's the first man I had any feelings for, after it happened. Other than Chip, who I already adored. He's been a father figure. Bill Cameron—well, he's gone back to Will now —*him*, I was angry with, of course, but now I could just eat him up with a spoon. I wish you could meet him and Eleanor. They are a hoot and a half."

"How old did you say they are?" The women walked out onto the porch and sat down to watch the firefly chase.

Kristina shook her head in amazement. "Early eighties, but you'd never know it. A year ago, Will thought he was dying, and now he's probably going to outlive us all. Love is powerful medicine."

Donna groaned. "I could sure use a dose right now."

In the semi-darkness, Jessica waved to the women. "Hey, I just had a thought. Why don't you come to Florida with us, Kristina? It's your spring break, too, right?"

Ian and Kristina lay in their bed downstairs staring up at the ceiling, their naked arms and legs wrapped around each other in a provocative pretzel. "Do you think they're asleep yet?" Ian whispered.

Kristina's silent giggle made her body shake in the dark. "I don't hear Angela anymore, so they're probably asleep. I think you wore her out, chasing her around the yard. Very clever of you." Her hand moved further down from Ian's smooth, muscled stomach. "Well, well, well. What have we got here?" Her hand circled his erection gently then squeezed him firmly.

Ian shifted in the bed to face her, moving her outside leg onto his thigh. "Surely, you know by now," he murmured. "That happens every time I'm next to you or see you walk across the room or hear your voice on the phone." Ian kissed her tenderly as she wriggled higher on the mattress, welcoming what she knew was his next move. "How will I live without you if you go to Florida?"

As he pulled her buttocks closer, his cock slid easily into her wetness. Foreplay was not usually as muted or prolonged as tonight while they waited for their guests to settle in, but it had aroused a different kind of excitement. As Ian entered her, Kristina stifled a moan.

Jessica lay on her back, in what had been Ian's bedroom, before Will and Eleanor reconnected, after being teenage lovers, and Will moved in with her, before Ian and Kristina fell in love. She listened to the quiet even breathing of Angela's slumber on a pallet Kristina had made on the floor at the foot of the bed using soft down comforters and colorful quilts.

"You'd be surprised how cool it gets at night," Kristina had warned. "The window's closed, but if you want to open it, be careful. Use the shim on the sill to hold it up, or it will come down with a slam. Don't let it catch your fingers."

Early for them to be in bed by usual standards, the women were ready to sleep after a stressful and tiring day. They had visited outside, gotten showers and baths, then sat and talked as they sipped hot cocoa and rocked Angela to sleep. When Donna carried Angela upstairs, the child had stirred, asking for a story. Donna had curled beside her, relating the story of a handsome stonemason who got hurt and how a beautiful princess helped him finish. "And they lived happily ever after." Soon, Angela slept soundly again as Donna climbed back under the covers with Jessica.

Jessica whispered, "I notice you didn't mention the princess' whip or handcuffs."

Donna giggled quietly. "What I wouldn't give for our red room right now. Or any room, for that matter, as long as Eric's in it."

"I feel your pain," Jessica said. "Worth is away on business now and then, but this is the first time I've left *him* behind."

Silence. Then Donna whispered, "Don't take this the wrong way, but couldn't you see Ian on the big screen?"

Jessica turned to face her friend with a low conspiratorial giggle. "Oh my, yes. A different kind of handsome than Worth or Eric, but wow. That hair, those muscles, that—"

"Ass," Donna interrupted. "Do you think they're asleep yet? I wouldn't be, I'll tell you that."

The women listened intently. "Was that a moan?" Jessica whispered. "I thought I heard a little moan."

Below their bed, a steady rhythm of muted sound began. The mattress didn't squeak, but the shifting of body against body, thrust against thrust, made a definite sound. The women listened, transfixed as they imagined what was happening below. As the rhythm grew faster, each discovered that her own hands had moved, and her eyes had closed vicariously. Instinctively, they turned so that they were back to back, missing their men acutely.

When Jessica and Donna thought they could bear the suspense no longer, a muted cry of delight was heard below them. The movements slowed to a halt and all was quiet again. All they could hear was the sound of their own accelerated heartbeats, their own heavy breaths, and Angela's soft inhalations from her pallet.

Jessica threw off the covers from her side of the bed. "Are you hot?" she whispered. "I'm hot. I'm going to open the window. What was that Kris said about a shim?"

Ian and Kristina snuggled in post-climactic bliss. Suddenly, they heard a sharp noise above them and a distinct "Ouch!" followed by loud shushing and softer movements. They tensed a little, picturing the scene. Someone had evidently opened the window then let it slam down on fingers. After a moment, all was quiet again.

"Do you think they heard us making love?" Kristina murmured.

"Maybe," Ian whispered. "Such a deal—dinner *and* a show."

4

Ian Has an Issue

Andy called Jessica at nine-thirty the next morning. "It was the battery," she said, managing to say it without even a hint of *I told you so.* "I checked everything else, and you're good to go."

They had eaten breakfast and packed already, adding Kristina's bag to the stack. Ian assured her that as much as he would miss her, she should go to Florida, relax, and spend time with her friends. He would hit the books while she was gone, knock out a few papers he had put off for his master's program.

"Once Donna reconnects with Eric," he added, "Jessica may need help with Angela." Kristina had told him how badly Donna was missing her husband.

That was the deciding factor. As much as she loved her niece, she saw what a handful Angela could be. Jessica had enough going on with her own pregnancy. The less stress, the better.

Ian kissed her goodbye so thoroughly that Jessica and Donna pulled Angela quietly outside to wait for them. A little chagrined, they both walked outside. "He's got to drive us in,"

Kristina explained, "or my car would just be sitting. I guess I get another goodbye kiss out of the bargain."

Within an hour, Jessica's SUV was packed once again. Jessica turned a movie on Angela's tablet while they readied for the trip. Sitting beside her niece, Kristina tapped her on the arm. "Whatcha watching, sweetie?"

"Bambi," she said. "I love Bambi."

"You sure seemed to last night," Kristina said with a chuckle, ignoring the inquisitive look on Angela's face.

Andy and Ian waved to the SUV until it was out of sight. "Do you have any other customers today?" Ian asked. The station was self-service. Lucy, a high school girl, manned the register inside. It wasn't as stocked as a convenience store, but locals relied on Pete's Place for essentials like fresh eggs and milk, beer, the mustard they forgot to bring on their way to the lake.

Andy shook her head. "Not that I know of. Lucy's got my number in case, but I think I'll head home and check on Daddy. Want to tag along? He might be up to a game of chess, you never know."

Ian shook his head. "I've got some school work to plow through, but how about I bring lunch after that? I'm working at The House, then I could come over." It briefly dawned on him that were it anyone but Andy, a woman might think he was flirting.

Andy waved as he got into his car. As she put her hands in her pockets, she suddenly remembered something and called for Ian to wait, leaning over to talk to him through the open window. "I wrote down the name of a shop in Orlando if Jessica runs into any more trouble. Honest guy, won't gouge her for having out-of-state plates. I meant to give it to her. Could you relay the information when you talk to Kristina later?"

He took the little slip of paper and assured her that he would, then drove off, chastising himself for fretting about flirtation. Andy wasn't like most young women. It occurred to him that he'd never known her to date. *Into girls? Asexual?* He couldn't relate to a person having no libido at all, but he'd better learn to, if he planned to go into social work. Empathizing with people of all kinds and inclinations would be important.

Andy stuck her head inside the door of the little store. "I'm heading home, Lucy. Call me if you need me!" As she turned to walk to her truck, however, she saw Jeffrey pedaling toward her. "What's up, buttercup?" she called.

"You know I do not like nicknames," he retorted, "especially when they don't make sense."

Andy rolled her big eyes. "It's s rhyme. Up. Buttercup."

"Oh," Jeffrey conceded. "I do like rhymes. My mother wants to know how Pete is doing."

"Why doesn't she call him?" This wasn't the first time this had happened. Thanks to the tower on Cameron Mountain, the whole area had good signals. *She has a phone. Why so shy with Daddy?* Last night's trip down memory lane must have stimulated odd, random thoughts, because a particularly surprising thought suddenly occurred to her. *Surely not.* "Does your mom talk about me much?"

Jeffrey concentrated, then shook his head. "Not much. I see you every day, just about, so when I tell her what I've done or who I've talked to, you're always in there somewhere. But she doesn't ask about you specifically. Once in a while, I guess. Last Tuesday. And the Thursday before that while we were folding laundry."

Andy smiled at her friend's specificity and amazing memory. "I just wondered."

Jeffrey nodded. "She talks about *Pete* all the time, though. Every day, lately. It started at eight-thirty last Sunday when she was making breakfast. We had pancakes, butter, syrup, and crisp bacon, the way I like it."

For once, Andy was pleased with the amount of detail. It could be annoying to listen to the litany of trivia but if Mama Wilson was getting sweet on her father, Jeffrey's excellent recall was a definite advantage. "What does she say?"

Even Andy was ill-prepared for the deluge of comments Jeffrey's mother had evidently made in the last week. Jeffrey put the kickstand down on his bike and crossed his arms. He took a deep breath and began. "'Pete Cummings is the nicest man in town. Pete Cummings is a smart businessman but also generous to the local folks. Pete Cummings was the cutest boy in class and one time we kissed at a school dance. Pete Cummings never should've married that wild girl who ran off with the band, but of course, that would have meant no Clyde, Chance or Andy and that would have been a terrible loss.'"

Andy held up her hands. "Enough. I get the idea! Jeffrey, has it occurred to you that your mom has a crush on my dad?"

"Of course, she has a crush on him. Anyone can see that. I was beginning to think you were never going to notice," Jeffrey said. "When they built that new gas station close to my house, she kept coming here. And she knows how to do a lot of things she asks him for help with, like that time she said the fuse had blown and could he change it for her." Jeffrey shook his head. "It's no surprise that as long as it took for *you* to notice, he hasn't noticed, either."

Andy gave her friend a hug. "Sorry about that. When I shaved my head, maybe it affected my brain too."

Jeffrey rubbed her scalp softly. "You're a little stubbly. May I shave it this time?"

"Sure. Put your bike in the truck. Let's go to my house now, check on Daddy, and you can shave my head. Then we need to plan. If we wait on Pete Cummings and Marilda Wilson, they'll *never* get together."

Ian rubbed his eyes. He often found it more productive to work on his classes at The House, what he called the Exagorà House. Unless there was a support group meeting or a counseling session in progress, it was usually quiet. In time, they hoped to offer things like exercise or films, but now, activities were limited.

Today, it was just Ian and a stack of textbooks. He hoped, with a master's degree in social work, he could help Cherokee youth at risk. As he rummaged through his pockets for a mint, he pulled out the paper Andy had handed him. Unfolding it, he was surprised by her distinctive penmanship. Neat, confident, but with a bit of artistry. Mentally reminding himself to call Kristina when he was through working, he flipped through the filing cabinet for a letter from one of his instructors that he had tucked away the last time he worked there.

We need to get this better organized, he thought as he went through the colorful file folders. Another sample of Andy's handwriting caught his eye. It was inside a folder for Exagorà House's support group, one that was to be confidential. It was just so shocking to see handwriting he recognized that he pulled the paper out without thinking. Unsigned and apparently anonymous, the penmanship could not have shouted "Andy Cummings" any louder. Ian's heart sank as he read the account of the near-rape of a fourteen-year-old girl by an unnamed minister. He would have been at the Indian school at the time, but he couldn't remember hearing any gossip about it in Poplar Gap. *This must have been a venting exercise. That poor girl.*

He would say nothing to her, or to Kristina, of course. Should he tell Helen? He resolved to "be there" for Andy, more than he had been in the past. Her brothers no longer lived close by; *he* could be a brother to her. He had known the Cummings since he was young, but what good was a social work degree if you didn't use it *for* good? Taking lunch to the house would be a perfect start.

When Ian tapped on the screen door to the Cummings' kitchen, he was surprised to hear Pete welcome him inside. "You must be feeling better," he said as he entered.

"Much better, thanks. Andy said you were coming with lunch. Awfully nice of you; just set it anywhere. Jeffrey's shaving her head in the bathroom, but they should be about done."

Pete Cummings had aged well. His dark hair had distinctive gray patches at the temples with gray sprinkled throughout. He had Andy's hazel eyes, but his facial features had been handed down more to his sons than to his daughter. No one would mistake him for a movie star, but he was muscular and trim, ate healthy, didn't smoke or drink to excess, and had a winning smile.

Ian had always liked Pete, but reading about the way he'd taken care of the preacher in his daughter's past raised his status considerably higher. "I'm glad you're feeling better. Andy can hold down the fort at the station, though. She just fixed the car of one of Kristina's friends from out of town."

Pete chuckled as he filled glasses with ice water for lunch. "She told me. People almost always think there's something exotic and tragically wrong with their cars, especially if they look it up on the Internet first. When a car doesn't start, it's almost *always* the battery. I've made more money off my time looking for what they just *knew* was the problem than on just about anything else."

"Andy said I did a good job," Jeffrey said, walking in.

Following him was the slickly shaven Andy, drying her head with a towel. "Something smells good."

Ian opened the bags and set containers on the table. " I thought we'd give that new Chinese take-out on Main a try."

The four of them chatted as they ate, then Andy cleared everything away and winked at Jeffrey. "Daddy, Marilda Wilson wondered if you might help her with something when you're feeling better. Looks like you are. Doesn't it look that way to you, Jeffrey?"

"What is it this time?" Pete asked, a little annoyed.

"Well, Daddy, does it matter?" Andy teased. "She needs *something*, and she wants *you* for the job. Apparently, no one else will do."

Pete frowned and let out a ponderous breath. "I guess now's as good a time as any. I'll take your truck since Jeffrey's bike's already in the back. Thanks for the grub, Ian. Come on, Jeffrey. Day's a-wasting."

Ian caught Andy's ghost of a headshake directed at her friend and raised his eyebrows as Jeffrey declined the offer.

"That's okay, Mr. C," Jeffrey said. "I've got things to do before I head home. I'll take my bike out, though."

Pete shrugged as Jeffrey walked outside with him. The room was suddenly quiet with just Ian and Andy there. They had never been alone in a room before. As Ian thought about it, he couldn't remember a time when he'd been alone with *any* female since Kristina came to the mountain.

It hadn't been a conscious effort. Blissfully ignorant of how his presence often affected women, Ian had accidentally managed to avoid any awkward situations. But now, knowing what Andy had gone through when she was fourteen, Ian was suddenly and acutely aware of his maleness, his size, how easy it would be to take advantage of her.

Ian cleared his throat. "I was working at The House earlier."

"Yeah? Anything going on today?"

"No."

There was a moment in which Ian was sure Andy had something on her mind, but it passed. "I guess I'd better go. For the first time in months, I'll have the cabin all to myself." Ian grimaced. "Can't say I'm looking forward to that. Say! Did I detect some monkey business afoot with all that Marilda-needs-you stuff?"

Andy leaned against the sink as she looked out the kitchen window, wrinkling her nose. "Was it that obvious?" She grunted. "I would love nothing more than for Daddy and Jeffrey's mom to hit it off. He's been alone a long time." As she turned to face the sink, she muttered, "Me too."

"What's that?"

"Nothing," Andy said brightly, returning to the table. "I used to think I'd always live here with Daddy, taking care of him. But that's selfish. He deserves better than that."

Ian's eyes clouded over with concern. "So do you." She looked so surprised, he immediately regretted it. "I'd better go. Be seeing you."

Andy couldn't concentrate on her book, threw it across the room, and then walked over and picked it up. "What is wrong with me?" she cried aloud. All she could think about was the way Ian looked at her after lunch, as if he were seeing her for the first time. No one had seen her, not like that, since George Sanderson. It was not a pleasant feeling. Maybe she should talk to him about it.

She'd planned to confront George one time and didn't—which hadn't ended well. Should she make it clear to Ian that as much as she liked him, she wasn't interested? Not just in him, in *any* man.

Which would be a lie, her inner self chided. *You loved the way it felt to be held by George Sanderson. To be kissed. To be wanted. You're just afraid you blew your only chance.*

Andy sighed. Maybe she should talk to Helen Hamilton. For this, though, she'd like a man's perspective. Ian was studying to be a social worker, she remembered. And now, without him in the same room being all manly and handsome and caring, she knew he hadn't meant anything. She looked at her reflection in the mirror. "Of course, he didn't mean anything," she told herself. "Why would he?"

5

An Interruption

I an laughed as Kristina described in great detail the trip south. They'd stopped to spend one more night on the road, planning to meet Eric at Disney World early the next day. Angela was getting cranky and the women were ready to stretch and relax a bit as well. He could hear the television in the background, and occasionally, other voices. Jessica had talked to Worth about sending someone to do a story on *Andy*, of all people!

"She's unique, that's for sure," Ian said, "but she may not want the notoriety. It would be up to her." He felt suddenly protective of his newly acquired "sister."

"Of course," Kristina said, wondering about his tone. She decided to ignore it, launching into her hilarious account of a carload of college boys they'd seen when they got back on a major highway. The guys had honked the horn excitedly as they slowed down in the lane beside the SUV. One of them had held up a sign that said *"Can we get a kiss?"*

"Donna was driving, and I was in the back, blocking their view of Angela's car seat." Kristina giggled. "So I bent over so they could see her while Jessica made a little sign to hold up that said, *"Taken, Old, & May We."*

"You're not old. Those boys had good taste," Ian said, rocking gently on the porch swing. "Every one of you ladies is a beauty."

Kristina sighed. "I miss you. This is the first night in so long I won't be sleeping with you."

"I miss you too. If you were here right now," Ian said softly, "you wouldn't be sleeping."

Kristina lowered her voice. "I don't have much privacy, so this will have to be one-sided, but Donna was talking about her sexy FaceTime calls with Eric. How about describing what we'd be doing?"

Ian closed his eyes. "Mmm. Let's see. Imagine we're here at the cabin. I'm sitting on the front porch, reading a book on the swing."

Kristina giggled. "*So* not sexy."

"Patience! I've never done this before. I'm reading. And you come out the front door. And you're naked."

"Go on. That's more like it." Kristina glanced around the room to make sure no one was paying attention to her.

"I'm on the swing, and you come out naked. I don't see you because I'm reading, but then you walk up to the swing and lean down to make it stop moving." Imagining the scene, he paused a second to adjust himself inside his jeans.

"Don't stop now! What are you doing?"

Ian chuckled. "If you must know, I've got a hard-on like you wouldn't believe. I had to shift."

Kristina took a deep breath. "What I wouldn't give…but go on, please."

"I'm on the swing reading and you stop the swing and you're naked. You take the book out of my hand and put my hands on your breasts as you straddle my lap. We kiss, and you reach down and unsnap my jeans and pull my enormous cock free."

"Mmm. 'Enormous.' It is, you know. And what about your underwear? I want details!"

"I'm not wearing underwear."

"That was smart. And sexy. What happens next?"

"Guess what? My jeans *are* unsnapped. Right now. And my enormous cock *is* standing here missing you."

Kristina gave a nervous little moan, whipping her head around to see if the others in the hotel room had noticed. "You're driving me wild, here," she whispered, hoping the television would cover her words.

"Now you pull up onto your knees so your breasts are in my face. I suck hard on your nipples and kiss them as you sit down on me. It feels so good. So much better than what my hand is doing right now."

"That's not fair! I can't do anything but listen," Kristina hissed.

"Well, you're the one who asked. How was I to know I'd get all hot and bothered. Oh, *shit*!"

A few hours from Orlando, Kristina heard the swing creak as Ian stood suddenly. The phone crashed to the porch and she heard muffled but frantic sounds of fumbling and zipping. Even though she knew he didn't have the phone to his ear, she kept saying, "What? What's the matter? What's going on?" until both Donna and Jessica called to her to see what was going on.

When she heard Ian's voice again, it was no longer husky. "Um, I'll talk to you later, okay? Someone's here."

Kristina frowned. "At the cabin? Now? It's almost dark." Her heart stopped as she heard a woman's voice in the background. "Who is it?"

"It's Andy. I-I'll call you later." *Click.*

Kristina lay awake beside the sleeping Angela trying to squelch her imagination. During Ian's phone call, her imagination had been most helpful, but now it was just annoying. She knew she was overthinking, but that didn't stop her. But really! She'd only lived in Poplar Gap seven months. She'd known Ian for even less time. They fell in love so fast. *Too fast? And the first fucking time I'm not in his bed, another woman shows up? I've never known anyone to drive all the way to the cabin to visit us, not outside of family.*

Her heart assured her there was a perfectly legitimate explanation, but her head wouldn't shut up. She slept fitfully, nightmares of college boys in cars putting drugs into her drink. It was sometime during the night when she woke in a cold sweat, realizing that Ian had neglected to call her back.

When Andy's truck pulled into the clearing, she saw Ian jump to his feet, hastily turn around and zip up his jeans? *Weird.* She parked and called to him as she got out of the truck. "Hey, stranger! I hope you don't mind a visit."

He picked up the phone, spoke a few seconds and put the phone in his back pocket. "Not at all. Not at all. What brings you to Cameron Mountain? We don't get many visitors, Kristina and I. She's not here."

Steady, fellow. "Yes, I know. That's why I'm here." She'd never seen Ian's face grow pale before. She tilted her head to one side and stared at him. "What the hell is wrong with you?"

Ian coughed and gestured to the rocking chairs. "Nothing. I'm sorry. I was on the phone with Kristina and you just surprised me."

They sat in silence for several awkward minutes before Andy said, "This is really nice up here. Peaceful."

"Yes. We love it. Kristina and I love it. And I love Kristina."

Ian looked so miserable that Andy laughed out loud.

"What?" he sputtered.

Andy nodded. "I get it. You're wondering why I'm here. I understand, amazingly enough. Mostly, I *never* understand what's going on with people, maybe from spending so much time with Jeffrey, who knows. But this afternoon after lunch, you said something about me deserving better, and for half a second, I thought it was a come on."

"It wasn't."

"Of course, it wasn't. This isn't, either."

Ian blew out a breath of relief. "Of course, it isn't. Can I get you something to drink?"

A moment later, when he handed her a cold beer, she pointed to his crotch. "So what were you and Kristina talking about that had you so worked up there?" Andy asked, her face blank.

He closed his eyes and made a face. "You saw?"

Andy laughed. "Hard to miss *that* big ole' thing," she said. "Hard, get it?" She got the giggles so much that tears were coming down her cheeks. She flapped her hands at him as she calmed down. "Sorry, I was raised with boys, remember? They didn't exactly protect my 'virgin ears'," she said, cupping her ears for effect. "Kristina's such a lady, you're probably shocked."

Ian chuckled in spite of the embarrassment. There was something refreshing about this extraordinary young woman. One minute, she was almost timid, the next, laughing raucously or saying something astonishing. "You *did* shock me, and that's hard to do." At the word again, they both burst out laughing.

Silence again. Then Andy sighed and shrugged her shoulders. "I need to talk to somebody." When Ian started to interrupt, she continued, "No, not your lady counselor. Helen's fine, and I've, well, I've been to a few of the support groups at Exagorà, but I've never really, I mean, I wrote something one time, but no one... You know my mama left when I was little. I have a difficult time trusting women because of it, I guess. Well, not Jeffrey's mom, but she's different."

Ian nodded. "I'm sure she'd understand whatever it is you want to talk about. Marilda Wilson's handled some har...I mean, some tough things in life."

Andy shook her head. "She wouldn't understand this. *I* don't understand this. What I'm feeling, that is. Oh, for fuck's sake, I'll just blurt it out." She looked at Ian with a determined stare. "When I was fourteen, an older man put the moves on me. And I liked it. I liked that he paid attention to me. It was like no one had ever seen me before, not as someone to be cherished. And touched. And kissed." Her voice, which had started so strong, was almost wistful now.

"But it was wrong," she said quietly. "Wrong of him, and wrong of me to like it." She laughed ruefully. "My first kiss. The first time I felt, um, wanted that way. But when he pulled out his, his..." She pointed again at Ian's crotch. "It scared the shit out of me. I'd never seen one, um, *hard*." Her eyes crinkled again. "I almost started laughing again." She smiled suddenly, that dazzling smile of hers. "It really does help to say it out loud. The others at group said it would, but I didn't believe them. I've never told anyone but Daddy, and I glossed over the details. He got the idea."

Ian cleared his throat. "I-is he still around? I've never seen your dad get angry, but I can imagine he didn't take the news well."

Andy looked up at the sky. Stars were just beginning to show, and fireflies danced in the yard. "He did not. Neither did my brothers." She paused. "The man left town during the night."

"The min—" Ian began and then stopped, his eyes widening.

"The what? I never said he was my minister." Andy's eyes narrowed. "Did Helen Hamilton *tell* you what I wrote? You want to see angry, you'll see angry when I get my fucking hands on her!" Andy burst into tears and put her head into her hands as her whole body shook.

Ian reached out and laid a calming hand on her back. "Shhh. No, she didn't tell me. I'm so sorry." He explained how he'd pulled out the paper with her handwriting and seen details before he realized what it was. "I should have stopped reading. I should have. I'm so sorry. I didn't want you to know I knew. I wouldn't have hurt you like that, not for the world. I'm so sorry you went through that."

Suddenly, he remembered the night he and Kristina had been snowed in, how she had opened up to him about her rape at college, how he'd reached out to her and the lovemaking that had resulted. He pulled his hand back as if he'd been burned, so sharply that Andy raised her head.

"What?"

"I-I shouldn't have touched you, Andy. It was in friendship, I promise."

Andy nodded sadly. "I know it was. Don't worry. I was mad about the paper, but I can see how it happened. And now that I see what talking about it does, how it feels, I think I'll be able to bring it up in group. Maybe. But I like that you know. Really." She frowned and sat up formally. "Which brings us to the reason for my visit."

Ian waited. "Do you want another beer or—"

Andy held up a hand. "I'm fine, thanks." She clucked her tongue. "I thought telling you about the preacher was going to be the hard part," she smiled, "but this is worse." She looked like the tears were about to start again but caught herself. "I keep telling myself that he was a fluke. A fraud. That he lied about his feelings and how special I was. That I believed a lie. But I want it to be true. I don't know."

"You *are* special, Andy," Ian said quietly. "You have to know that."

"Do I? My own mama left when I was practically a baby. I've been raised rough and tumble. Oh, I know it's so fucking 'special' to be the only girl in town who can switch out spark plugs or assemble an engine, but look at me!" She pulled at her overalls. "You'd never even know there's a woman in here."

Ian chuckled. "That's easily remedied. Wear something different."

"You'd think it would be that simple, but honestly, I've worn this, this fucking *uniform*, for so long, I wouldn't know where to start. People will talk."

Ian raised his eyebrows. "More than they talk about you shaving your head or frequently saying 'fuck'?"

Andy rubbed her scalp, grimacing. "I am glad I did it, but it *was* a bit extreme, wasn't it?"

"A bit."

"Mama Wilson says I'm prettier than Persis Khambatta, whoever that is."

"Mama Wilson is correct," Ian said. "I've seen that movie. You make Persis Khambatta look like a boy."

Andy blushed. "People think Jeffrey and I are weird, don't they?"

Ian shook his head. "Different. Not weird." He tilted his head from side to side. "A little weird. But in a good way."

Andy rose abruptly and began to pace. "We're not lovers, you know. People have thought that too. I'm not sure Jeffrey even thinks that way about *anyone*, but he damn sure doesn't think that way about me, and I damn sure don't think that way about him."

Ian watched her pace, as antsy as a cat in a roomful of

rocking chairs, Chip might say. "What do you want, Andy? Out of life, I mean."

Andy stopped and put her hands on her hips. "I want a *man*! I want sex! I want kissing! I want to see the world beyond Humphrey! But how will that ever happen? It's not even realistic to *want* those things, much less make them happen. I know, I know," she said with a nod, rolling her eyes as she sat down. "I should just settle for taking care of Daddy and the shop and—"

Ian reached over and grabbed her hands in his, hoping for the right words that would comfort a sister. "You will not settle, Andrea Cummings. Not on my watch. And that's a promise."

6

Old Insecurities

Jessica and Donna were getting a crash course in Old Kristina. She had slept fitfully, she said, that was why she was so cranky. Which was true. She'd lain in bed beside Angela, staring at the ceiling of the hotel room. She had only met Ian a few months before. What did she really know about him? He was handsome as all get out, and charming, but what about his past? His character?

To pass the time and be productive, she'd mentally gone through every counseling session with Elizabeth that she remembered, the exercises in mindfulness, not letting circumstances and the behavior of others control her. Breathe deeply. Four seconds in. Hold. Four seconds out. It was no use. *We never had visitors outside the family and now 'Miss-May-I-Lube-That-For-You-Mister' shows up?*

For a long time after Kristina was drugged and raped by three college boys at a fraternity party, waking up alone, outside, no longer a virgin, she had struggled with her identity, her feelings of self-worth. Her sister Layla's crisis with a premature delivery had galvanized her into positive action, finding a counselor. Elizabeth had helped her immensely. The move to

Poplar Gap, making friends, falling in love, had it all been for nothing? Was it all just to pull her down again, to break her heart and her will?

It hadn't helped matters that Jessica was excited about pitching a story on Andy to Worth for the national magazine. It had sounded like a big deal when she'd called Worth earlier. Great story, great photos, beautiful artwork, blah, blah, blah. Hopefully Disney would be so jam-packed, she wouldn't have to hear her gush about the woman her boyfriend was cheating with. *You don't know that. Shut up.*

Kristina was not good at hiding her misery. Although she apologized several times for her negativity, she also knew it was up to her to pull herself out of it. Elizabeth and Ian were the only people she'd really opened up to other than Layla, but she was feeling pretty desperate. "I'm just so worried about Ian," she finally said. The four of them were standing in line at the entrance to Disney World. Eric hadn't arrived yet.

Jessica and Donna exchanged a look. "He obviously loves you very much," Jessica said. "What little time we spent around him, that much was clear. Why the sudden concern?"

"Our phone call last night was cut short when *Andy Cummings* drove up." When the women said nothing, she explained that no one came to the cabin but family. *No one.* "I was gone for only a few hours and she suddenly makes the trip? Something's fishy."

Donna picked Angela up and moved forward in line a few paces as the gate opened far ahead. "Don't you think he would have tried to hide it if he'd planned for her to visit? Logic dictates that he was surprised by the sight of her too."

"That's a good point," Jessica chimed in. "I agree. Ian didn't know she was coming."

"For a journalist, I think that's a poor choice of words under the circumstances," Kristina sulked and then widened her eyes. "Her very *name* is Cummings." She groaned, then rolled her eyes. "I know, I know. My head tells me there's nothing going on, but my heart is only just now healing. I felt inadequate and unworthy for so long. I don't want to lose that, you know? He said he'd call me later. And he didn't."

Jessica nodded. "With Worth and me, it was a constant roller coaster ride for a while. I wasn't sure *what* the hell was going on. I'd be all excited that he felt as strongly as I did, and then he'd act so prim and proper, I thought I'd explode." She patted her stomach. "And look how well *that* turned out. Now I look like I'm *really* about to explode. I can't believe this kid's got four more months to grow. Where? How will something that big fit inside me?"

Donna laughed lasciviously. "That was the trouble to start with, letting something big fit inside—"

"You behave when you're holding my niece!" Jessica laughed, slapping playfully at her friend's arm.

"Speaking of being inside someone." Donna waved frantically at the sight of Eric walking toward them from the parking lot. His longish hair was pulled back into a ponytail, and he wore cargo shorts, sandals, and one of his floral "Florida" shirts. Seeing her, he broke into a jog as Donna handed Angela to Kristina and ran to meet him.

People in line stopped looking at their watches and the line to stare at their passionate embrace off to one side. One woman punched her husband's arm and said loudly enough for others to hear, "Why don't you ever kiss *me* like that?"

"Humph," the man retorted. "Why don't *you* ever run to meet me?"

The line moved forward a little as Eric and Donna continued to kiss. "It's been too long, babe," he murmured in her ear, nibbling it gently.

Donna sighed deeply, realizing suddenly how public their embrace was. She pulled away slightly, allowing only a narrow space between them. "Do we *really* have to spend the day going on rides?" She leaned in and whispered, "I only want to ride you."

Eric grinned. "My place is only about twenty minutes away."

Jessica, watching them from the line, was not surprised when Donna whipped around, shrugged, and waved goodbye before they took off at a snappy pace to the parking lot. She patted Angela on the back. "Looks like it's just the three of us for the day," she sighed, "and I don't blame them a bit."

"When are you due?" Kristina asked.

The line was moving forward a little more quickly now. "June, if all goes according to plan," Jessica said. "So far, so good. When's the wedding?"

Kristina made a face. "We were talking about August, before school starts. But now—"

"Oh good grief," Jessica said, frustrated. "*One* thing has happened. *One*. Probably not even a *big* thing. Andy may've had a good reason to be there, and he simply forgot to call. Don't dwell on it until you know for sure, okay? Andy doesn't seem like the type to run after a guy. I wasn't sure *she* wasn't a guy when I first saw her."

Kristina set Angela down and took her hand. "Don't let go, Angel. We're almost there. I'm trying, Jess. Really, I am. Maybe Mickey Mouse will take my mind off things."

Donna giggled as Eric drove, it seemed to her, faster than usual. He was living in a guest cottage tucked behind the main house in an exclusive gated community, where he was doing stone work. He had sent photos of the lush landscaping, estates, lakes, and parks, but none of that factored into Donna's present anticipation. "I'm about to slide right off my seat, I'm so ready," she said. "I still can't believe you're here and I'm here. After two long months!"

Eric drew in a breath and looked over lovingly at her. "This is the last time, Donna. If I take another job like this, you're coming with me. If Worth won't give you the time off, you can get another job. I'm serious." He took his right hand off the steering wheel to play at Donna's blouse, untying the string at the neckline and tickling her breasts underneath the gauze fabric. With his eyes safely on the road, he continued huskily, "I appreciate the FaceTime, I do, but it's not the same. This is it, understand? No more separations."

Donna smiled and saluted. "Aye, aye!" When they had first become intimate, Eric had been enthusiastically content with being sub to her Domme, but in time, he'd realized that she needed more from him. As exciting as their sexual games had been for him with her in the dominant role, he had found even more pleasure taking it over himself. Occasionally, they switched things up, but they had learned to put a priority on complete communication.

"Have you looked into any clubs around here? Don't get me wrong…" she shifted her weight so that she could massage his crotch with her foot, "…anywhere is fine with me, the way we always say—"

Eric smiled. "Anywhere, anytime, any way, but only you. I think you'll be pleased with my, um, furnishings. The maid who comes in tomorrow may raise her eyebrows, but I don't care."

Donna sighed, pressing her bare foot more forcefully against his erection. "I wish I could stay more than two nights, but Layla was adamant about how much time Angela could be gone. Honestly, I don't get it. It's the first time she and Keith have been alone for more than an evening since Angela was born. I'd be hungrier than that."

Eric stopped tracing his finger along Donna's breast to massage her foot, kneading every inch firmly, the way she liked it. "Having children changes the dynamics, babe. Keith's mentioned it quite a bit to me and Worth, to his dad, when you ladies are off in baby mode. I'm not in any hurry." He glanced over at Donna to gauge her reaction. "I want us to have a family, but maybe in a few years."

Donna smiled. "I agree. One day." She removed her foot and reached over to unzip the zipper on his shorts. "Not today."

For the next few minutes, Donna held his cock in her mouth, sucking, biting gently, licking along its shaft, circling him with her fingers, and tracing the head with her tongue. The car he'd borrowed from his employer for the day was, fortunately, a Range Rover, both plush and spacious. Donna was enjoying pleasuring him orally so much that, at first, she didn't realize the vehicle had slowed to a stop. She popped her head up, surprised to discover that they were in a secluded area. "Where are we?"

Eric shook his head as he pressed the button to lower the windows and turned the key off. The orange grove appeared to be empty of anyone but them, and Donna could hear the breeze rustle through the trees. The air was sweet with the aroma of orange blossoms and filled with the low-pitched sound of beating wings as countless insects zeroed in on waiting nectar.

"If I hadn't stopped, we'd probably have had an accident. You were driving me wild, babe." Eric slipped his shorts down. "No one will see us. I want you now." Donna continued to turn her head this way and that for signs of workers in the rows of trees. "I said *now*." Eric reached over and pulled her blouse off roughly as she wriggled out of her shorts and panties. Eric adjusted the seat to give her more room as he pulled her on top of him. "Fuck foreplay," he murmured. "*Now. Fuck me*."

Donna slid onto him and pressed her breasts into his waiting lips as she began to rock gently. Eric's hands moved to her buttocks and drew her closer with all of his strength. *You want it rough? I'll give it to you rough.* Sliding her feet to the floor of the car, she lifted her weight off of him, then pushed hard with her feet as she rose up and down as quickly as she could, grasping the headrest with both hands and arching her back, inwardly thanking the car's designers for making it possible to get this much leverage. She thrust harder and harder as Eric's cries grew louder and louder. When he climaxed, she brought her knees to the generous seat for a few seconds before stretching out again, this time rocking gently. "My turn," she whispered.

Eric responded by leaning her back so that he could caress her breasts. He took a nipple in each hand, fingers squeezing firmly as she pressed into him. He kissed her neck, her shoulders, took one breast into his mouth, and then the other as she breathed in the sweet aroma from the blossoms. Her eyes closed as the wave of ecstasy built ever so slowly. Donna's hips picked up speed as Eric grasped them. Joined as one being, they rode the wave together, him, relishing her orgasm as she had relished his.

Donna relaxed and collapsed her naked body against his chest, inhaling the scent of his perspiration. Outside the Range Rover, bees buzzed. Leaves stirred. Far away, a tractor's engine started. The sun was climbing in the sky and all was again well.

After a few minutes, Donna whispered, "So what will we do for the rest of the day?"

When Kristina, Angela and Jessica emerged from the darkness of Peter Pan's Flight, into the noonday brightness, Kristina pulled out her phone. "I thought I felt a vibration. Huh! I've got four missed calls from Ian."

Jessica steered the group toward a bench. "Told you so.

There's nothing to worry about. I'll take Angela to the bathroom while you call him." As Kristina took a seat, Jessica gave instructions. "Don't be shy about telling him you don't appreciate the forgotten call last night or letting him know you were upset. Good communication is not overrated."

Kristina listened to the ringing as Jessica and Angela zigzagged through the mass of people. *Is he at the cabin, in the truck, or…with Andy?* When it went to voicemail, she ended the call without leaving a message. She checked her call log. He'd tried to call just a few minutes earlier. She crossed her arms in defiance and sat back on the bench, oblivious to the sea of happy humanity moving in all directions. *So much effort and beauty into designing this place, so much talent. And all I can think of is Ian. And Andy. She's an artist, that one.* She should be doing something grand with her life, not repairing cars. Or stealing boyfriends. Kristina glanced to her right.

Tomorrowland's skyline loomed. *Where will I be tomorrow, and the next week, the next few months, the next year?* Mentally, she answered each question, Orlando, home, preparing for a wedding, living on the mountain with her husband. What had seemed so certain when she kissed Ian goodbye the day before, felt painfully elusive now. All the old feelings of being soiled, used, unworthy and unattractive—constant companions for many months after the frat party—knocked on the door of her mind once more.

"Mind if I sit? My feet are killing me."

Kristina looked up. A distinguished man, maybe in his sixties, stood in front of her. Worth once said that all bald men with beards look alike and she could see his point. This man wore a protective hat against the Florida sun, but his neat goatee and mustache did indeed make him a brother of Worth, even though grayer. "Of course not, go right ahead."

The man took a seat with a sigh and a smile and nodded toward a nearby shop. "Our tenth anniversary," he said. "That store was so frilly, I could feel my life force being sucked dry." He chuckled. "Thanks for letting me perch for a moment." He looked up at the crowd intently. "They probably think I'm a dad sitting here with my beautiful daughter."

Kristina blushed. There was nothing flirtatious in his tone, merely frank appreciation. "Thank you, kind sir. Happy anniversary! May you be married many more." *Just ten years, so not a first marriage? Divorced? Widowed?*

For a second, the man's face clouded, then recovered. He sighed. "Funny thing about being around strangers all day, isn't it? I say things I'd never say to people I know well." He looked at Kristina frankly. "We're celebrating the tenth anniversary of our *love*, not our marriage. Circumstances, well, they do not permit us to be married, sadly. *Happily*, we have made the best of it."

A pretty woman with shoulder-length gray hair approached, holding up two bags in triumph. "Mission accomplished!" she said as she joined them on the bench, pushing the man closer to Kristina. "Good call on the bench, love. It was a madhouse in there. You would've curled up in a little ball and started sucking your thumb if you'd stayed much longer." She leaned over and kissed the man easily, as if kissing him on benches was her favorite activity in all the world.

Kristina was about to introduce herself when Jessica and Angela returned. Angela grabbed her hands and pulled as hard as she could. "Dumbo, Aunt Krissy."

Smiling at the couple beside her, she rose. "Duty calls. Happy anniversary," she said.

Jessica looked at the couple over her shoulder. About the age of her mother and stepfather, this couple looked every bit as much in love as they were. "I hope Worth and I are that lovey-dovey when we're that age."

Kristina said nothing, considering the man's explanation. *Unable to marry each other, so probably still married to others,* she surmised. Which meant being separated *most* of the time, without damage to their relationship. As she walked, she took her phone out of her shoulder bag again and tried Ian's number.

This time, he answered right away, immediately apologetic. "I'm so sorry, Kristina. Andy's visit threw me for a loop yesterday, coming out of nowhere like that. We had a few beers and I went to sleep—"

"Alone?" she asked casually, but there was an edge in her voice that Ian could hardly miss.

To his credit, Ian did not snap a retort but adopted a soothing tone. "Of course, alone," he said. "Andy stayed about an hour. It was a good talk, actually."

Kristina couldn't muster a grain of enthusiasm, but she was determined to keep an open mind. "That's nice. Really. What did you talk about?" She lagged a bit behind Jessica and Angela, meandering through the throng. When they reached the ride, she motioned to Jessica to go ahead without her. *Ian,* she mouthed, pointing to the phone.

Managing to find a bit of privacy off to one side of a building, she mentally prepared herself for the detailed account that would put her mind at ease.

Instead, Ian hesitated. "I'm not sure how much she'd want me to repeat. I mean, I don't *think* she'd mind me telling you, but ethically, I should ask her first."

Kristina was momentarily speechless. "I see." A vision of the happy couple on the bench, joyful under less-than-ideal circumstances came to mind, but she pushed it aside. "So you get a visit from a single woman five seconds after I've left town, and now you're keeping her secrets?" Kristina was livid. "I certainly wouldn't want to offend the town's best mechanic, even if she is as bald as some of the tires she changes." She heard the bitchiness but couldn't control herself. "I hope you two have lots of good talks while I'm away. Goodbye!" *Click.*

When Ian tried to call back the next second, she declined and turned her phone off. *Let him deal with silence for once.*

Kristina joined the spectators, waving and smiling at the mix of adults and children high above them in sixteen molded elephants. *Elizabeth would tell me that my anxiety is robbing me of the joy of this moment.* She closed her eyes, trying to erase any mental images that interfered with the fun of being with Jessica and Angela in this glorious, happy place.

All she could see was Ian. With Andy.

7

Reese Takes an Assignment

W orth Vincent pressed his assistant's corresponding button on the intercom on his desk. Jessica was excited about the human interest story in Humphrey. He'd been there himself at Thanksgiving, forcing the Exagorà Foundation and its miscreant sons into a confrontation with Kristina Edwards, but he hadn't spent enough time in the town to be impressed.

What impressed Worth were results, and his mission had been a success. The former college boys had confessed to drugging and raping Kristina, but they were also truly sorry, he felt. The statute of limitations having run out, the apologies had been a start, sweetened by an annual grant for Kristina to use at her discretion. Jessica had told him about Exagorà House and numerous improvements at Kristina's school, thanks to the money.

And she'd told him about the bald mechanic with big eyes and a flair for painting. Interesting, certainly. Had Jessica not been his wife, he might not have acted so quickly, but she was. In addition, she had a reputation for good instincts. His own life was proof of that. She'd dug into something from his childhood and freed him of the weight it had caused. He owed her. If she wanted a story on this girl, he would oblige.

"You rang?" Skip's voice chirped.

"Who've we got who's free to travel? A week, maybe more, all expenses paid. Someone who could get the art also."

Skip made thinking noises. "Reese Maverick does good work. He's young but capable." *And cute as a button,* Skip thought.

"Send him in, please."

"Ten-four, good buddy."

A few minutes later, Reese stepped into Worth's office and, when invited to do so, sat down across from the editor. Hired by Worth's predecessor about the same time Jessica had started working at the magazine, he'd proven himself to be reliable. Nothing flashy, but dependable.

"How comfortable are you with a camera, Reese?"

The young man shrugged. "I have a good camera, which is half the battle. I'm not the star Paul is, but I manage. I've been doing more since that Lance character left, but you haven't hired anyone else yet so— "

The "Lance character" had, in fact, been a criminal Peeping Tom, now sitting in a cell. Worth sighed at the mention. "I planned to replace him and was looking for recommendations from Paul, but then you stepped up. You've done good work for us both as a writer and a photographer." He was not enjoying Jessica's time away from him and hoped to avoid breaking up anyone else's marital rhythm. "You don't have a family, do you? Single?"

"Currently," Reese said with a smile. "I'm engaged to a woman in New York I met last summer. The long distance relationship hasn't been ideal, but, um, well worth it."

Worth chuckled. "I'm glad it's working. But I didn't bring you in here to discuss your personal life, really. I'd like to send you on assignment. Little town called Humphrey, North

Carolina. There's one woman in particular I'm interested in. I've got her name, where she works, right here."

"What's her story?"

"To be honest with you, I'm sketchy on the details. My fault, not Jessica's. She was regaling me with details in one ear on the phone while I tried to answer some pressing matters my mother had emailed me. You know Molly."

He did. Molly owned the magazine and although not there often, her visits were memorable. Reese had often wondered if his fiancée might be cut from the same cloth—beautiful, sophisticated, wealthy, and demanding.

Worth continued. "She works at a shop, I'm sure of that. And she's a gifted artist. I think she said she was bald, but that may be wrong—it *sounds* wrong, anyway. Jessica thinks she'd make a great human interest piece for the national edition, our trial run. There's so much gloom and doom these days, I'd love the chance to break through with some sunshine." He grimaced. "I sound like the advertising department, sorry."

Reese pulled out his phone and opened his calendar app. "When do I leave?"

"As soon as possible. Down there, it would be 'I reckon.'" Worth chuckled. "We were there a few days in November—it's a lovely place, slower, friendlier. If Humphrey's bald woman can help us spread some of that further afield, I'd say we've done our jobs."

Reese made a face as he checked the dates. "I told my fiancée I'd meet her this weekend, but she'll understand. I can leave tomorrow."

Worth stood to shake his hand. "Great! Get with Skip for the details. Oh, and tell Paul to reassign anything you had going for the next week or so."

Paul, the magazine's main photographer, was Skip's husband. For Reese, who had never worked closely with a gay man before, the experience had been both educational and enjoyable. Paul was a gifted photographer and fun to be around. Now his education was expanding further. Reese had never been to the south, had never been sent out on a lengthy assignment, and had certainly never talked to a bald woman.

Should be interesting, he thought as he punched in Cammie's number. Camille Bentley was not going to be pleased. Reese drew in a breath. *If you look up "high maintenance" in the dictionary, Cammie's picture is on display.*

"Hi, honey," Reese said as he navigated his way through the magazine's main room filled with numerous cubicles, back to the photography section. "I'm afraid I have bad news."

Pete Cummings stood on the neat front porch of the Wilsons', noting the colorful flowers sitting here and there in pots, appreciating the soft melody of a wind chime that moved gently in the spring breeze, and cleared his throat. *Might as well get it over with.* He knocked on the screen door.

Marilda Wilson opened the door within seconds. They had been classmates throughout school. He had married just out of high school, but she had waited, marrying someone she met while working one summer in Asheville. Pete recalled that the Wilsons had been a happy couple, excited about the birth of their son Jeffrey. All of that had come crashing down with the diagnosis of autism when Jeffrey was four. Jeff Wilson, Sr. couldn't handle it. He simply left.

Marilda rented out rooms, cut financial corners, applied for assistance, whatever she could do to stay with Jeffrey until he was old enough to start school, then she'd worked diligently to provide for him. Jeff, Sr. helped off and on. He visited off and on. There had been less of that as the years passed.

For the last ten years, Marilda had been the office manager for the town's dentist, finally earning a good salary. Pete wondered why she didn't just call a contractor for whatever the problem was and not bother a man on his day off.

"Hi, Pete," Marilda said with a smile. "I'm so pleased you're feeling better. Was it a cold, your back, what?"

Pete grunted as he went inside, surprised afresh at what a woman's touch could do. If he'd let Andy decorate, who knew what kind of things *she'd* do. He was still embarrassed by the paintings she'd done for Exagorà House, but Marilda's parlor, as she called it, was feminine without being what Andy would disdain as *froufrou*.

"That new?" Pete asked, pointing to a beautiful ecru afghan of intricate design draped on the back of the floral sofa.

Marilda beamed. "I'm impressed you noticed. You haven't been here for a while. I started it during the big snow, when there wasn't much else to do. Just finished it last month."

"It's nice. You do good work." There was an awkward silence, two old friends with much to say but no words to say it with. Finally, Pete spoke. "What did you need help with?"

"Have a seat, Pete," Marilda said. "May I get you a glass of iced tea?"

"Sure." He sat on the sofa, glad he hadn't been in the shop that morning. *No grease to worry about soiling her pretty things.* "I offered to bring Jeffrey, but he said he had things to do before he came home," he called to the kitchen as he heard her open and close various doors and drawers.

Marilda brought out a pitcher of tea and two glasses, pouring one for him and then one for herself. She sat down beside him on the sofa. "Pete," she said, after taking a sip. "We've known each other a long time."

"Sure have. Remember Mrs. Felton in the first grade? She used to tell those awful stories at nap time." He laughed softly and took a long drink.

"I had nightmares about that poor woman drowning in the

lake," Marilda said quietly. "I was relieved when Mrs. Felton retired."

The silence fell again. Again, Pete spoke first. "You were always good about rope climbing and running fast. You could outrun all the boys by the time you were in high school."

"Maybe I ran too fast," Marilda said demurely. "No one caught me 'til that summer in Asheville." She put her glass on a little coaster on the coffee table and folded her hands in her lap. "Pete Cummings, I always thought highly of you. I think you know that. And we've both been alone for all these years." Tears welled up in her eyes as she continued. "I could have turned bitter and resentful because of Jeffrey, or because Jeff, Sr. left us, but I didn't. I could've died from cancer, but I didn't."

Pete pulled a clean handkerchief from his pocket and handed it to her to wipe her eyes. "You're a strong woman, Marilda, always have been. No one who knows you would ever think otherwise."

Marilda nodded as she blew her nose. "I'll wash this before I give it back, Pete. Yes, I'm strong. The good Lord has given me the strength I've needed, but there's something to be said for acknowledging weakness, too."

Pete was genuinely worried and stared at her. It was the first time he'd really looked at her in, well, forever. He saw her thin face and arms, the colorful scarf around her head. Chemo had not been completely kind to her, even as it saved her life. "The cancer's not back, is it?"

Marilda smiled, and Pete noted the little wrinkles at the corners of her eyes, the dimples created in her cheeks. For a second, he saw her as her younger self.

"No. It's not that," she said. "I've just realized that life is too short to not speak clearly about things. Maybe Jeffrey taught me that, I don't know. He is *painfully* honest." She paused as her bright eyes met Pete's. "I think he's onto something, though.

We *aren't* promised another day. I don't want to waste another minute of whatever time I have left."

Pete was visibly relieved. "That's a good way to look at things, Marilda. We'd all be happier if we lived like that. It's not always easy for folks to say what they want to say."

"No." Marilda sniffed. "I'll just say it, then, and you can do with it what you want." She stood and walked behind the wing back chair across from him, as if to shield herself from what might come. Placing her hands on the back of the chair, she blew out a breath and said, "I'm lonely, Pete. I haven't had anyone in my life except for Jeffrey since his father left. That's over ten years, Pete. Ten years without a man's arms around me, or in my bed."

She stopped, seeing his face. "Oh, don't look so shocked, Pete Cummings. We're grownups. I'm not propositioning you, I'm telling you that if you'd like to spend some time with me and see what happens, I'm willing."

Pete said nothing.

Stiffly, Marilda straightened her back and walked to the door. "I'm sorry that I bothered you, Pete. I'll not be bothering you again."

Pete sat on the sofa, looking around the room, taking in the details. Photographs of Jeffrey, many with Andy, documented his growth. Fresh flowers filled a vase on the little dining table between the parlor and the kitchen. Everything was clean, though well-worn. How difficult it must have been for a single woman to create this peaceful, beautiful home for a handicapped child without a man working alongside her. And then to face cancer, afraid of what might happen to her child, fighting because of him, more than anything.

He'd been treading water all these years. Rejected by his wife, he had walled himself off from any but his own children. He'd gone through the motions of playing cards with his buddies or going fishing with them, or tipping his cap to the ladies in town, but no one had touched his heart. He hadn't let them. Until this moment.

Pete nodded his head and stood, as if he agreed with her. When he reached the door, however, he looked down at her. "You were always such a pretty girl," he said softly. "I just hadn't looked in such a long time." Lifting her chin with one calloused hand, he bent down and kissed her softly on the lips and stood tall again, hoping he hadn't overstepped. This was uncharted territory for him, and he had no idea what to expect, or what was expected of him.

Marilda looked up at him with clear blue eyes and raised an eyebrow. "I think you can do better than that, Pete Cummings."

Closing the front door with one hand, Pete wrapped Marilda in an embrace that allowed all the built-up need and hurt to fuel a very different kind of kiss. Their shared passion surprised them both as tongues and hands explored hungrily, finally freed from years of solitude.

When they finally released, Marilda chuckled. "I feel a mite dizzy."

Pete led her gently back to the sofa, then he sat beside her. With a twinkle in his eye, he stroked her face lovingly. "Now," he said huskily, "where were we?"

"He said what?" Andy was adding oil to the lawnmower in back of the house when her phone rang.

It was Lucy, from the store. "Some man wants to interview you for a magazine article. Said you met the wife of the editor here. Fixed her car. Jessica Something."

"Vincent?"

"Yeah, that's it," Lucy said, popping her gum. "He'll be in town tomorrow or the next day and wants to take some photographs, spend some time with you. He sounded hand-some. And rich."

"How does one *sound* handsome and rich?"

Lucy giggled. "Well, he did. Just an FYI." *Click.*

Andy fastened the fill cap more tightly than usual. *A man wants to talk to me. Take photos of me. Shit, he'll take one look and burn rubber hightailing it out of town. Then again,* she thought, *it might be fun. Maybe even be good for the shop, for the town.* She could take him to Exagorà House, introduce him to the Camerons, the mayor, maybe Ms. Clark at the school.

Andy wiped her hands on her overalls and pulled the rope to start the mower. She'd have plenty of time to mow the yard before supper. Her father had said he'd do it after going to the Wilsons, but that was hours ago. Andy smiled. Maybe he and Mama Wilson had hit it off, after all.

8

Sudden Changes

Saturday afternoon, Ian Cameron and Andy Cummings ate lunch at East of Shanghai Chinese restaurant on Main Street as Jessica dropped Kristina off at Exagorà House. She had hoped Ian might be there working on his master's but figured she could relax there until he came to get her. He had tried to call numerous times, but she had still been pouting. Unreasonably, she fumed today, when she tried to call *him* and didn't get an answer.

Jessica shook her head as she showed Angela to the restroom inside. "Good grief, Kris. He's called you so many times, I lost count. Try again in a bit."

Kristina shrugged. "I was so bitchy the last time we talked, it's no wonder he's not thrilled to talk to me. But seriously, how well do we know each other? Don't you think it's at least possible that he and Andy might be up to no good? He's a man; she's a woman. Granted, she could use some help *looking* like one, but—"

"The bitchiness continues," Donna said dryly. She wasn't in the best mood herself, but oh, those few days and nights with

Eric. Well worth the trip, she told the others—so many times, they finally told her to shut up already.

Angela returned, looking this way and that. "Pretty flowers," she said.

Jessica herded Angela back outside before she started asking questions, not that she was *old* enough to recognize things, but knowing her..."Time to hit the road again. Mommy and Daddy miss you!" To the women, she added quietly, "And Aunt Jess is ready for a break!"

Kristina watched them pile into the SUV, grateful her road trip had ended but apprehensive about seeing Ian again. *Where could he be?* She called Chip, Eleanor, and Ian's grandfather. Everyone thought he was in town working. She waved goodbye as the SUV drove off, then decided to try again. *Hi, this is Ian. I'm not here, but if you'll leave a message.*

You're there, damn it, you're just not answering. Frowning, Kristina looked up the number of Pete's Place, hating herself for it. She was tired and wanted to go home, however, even if it meant finding out more than she wanted to, she had to try. *If Ian's there, I'll kill him, but I'll kill him after I've had a good soak in the tub.*

"Oh, hey, Miss Edwards," Lucy said between gum pops. "Ian? No, I haven't seen him. Want me to ask Pete?"

"Is Andy there?"

"No, ma'am, she said she was going to eat Chinese about twenty minutes ago. Sorry, got a customer." *Click.*

Kristina sighed. The Chinese restaurant was just down the street and she was suddenly hungry for more than answers. With her luggage inside, she locked the door, muttering to herself as she walked to the restaurant.

She saw them through the plate glass window, chatting easily and laughing. She stopped on the sidewalk and watched in horror as Andy offered Ian a bite of her food from her chopstick. *Oh no, you don't.*

When she opened the door, a little bell rang. Ian and Andy

looked her way with differing reactions. Andy smiled her usual smile; Ian was surprised. *They don't even have the decency to look guilty.*

Glaring at them, she said nothing but placed a take-out order at the counter before walking to their booth.

Andy spoke first. "How was Disney?"

Kristina was taken aback by her manner, as if there was absolutely nothing odd about her being at lunch with another woman's boyfriend. "It was fun," she said evenly. "Angela's a little young to appreciate it, but she had a grand time. Jessica and I were worn out. Two days of Disney is quite a work-out."

"What about—oh, I forgot the other woman's name. Short, curly blonde?" Andy returned to her egg roll, taking an enormous bite, then grinning. "Sorry, I eat like a fucking guy, don't I? Comes from those brothers of mine." She flashed another dazzling smile. "You know how men can be."

"I'm learning," said Kristina dryly as a server handed her a take-out bag, but she answered the question. "*Donna* preferred her husband's company to ours, and who can blame her?" She directed an icy look in Ian's direction. "Eric has long, sun-bleached hair and a full beard. Very handsome. Very sexy."

Ian's eyes narrowed just slightly as the arrow of her intent found its mark. "Welcome home." Ian slid over in the booth to make room for her. "Sit down, Kristina. Please. Join us. You must be hungry after the drive."

"No thank you," Kristina said crisply. "I'm heading to the cabin now. Chip 's giving me a ride since you were too busy to answer." She pivoted on one heel and marched out the door.

Once out of sight of the restaurant, she called Chip again. He was at Ellen's, she knew, and yes, he could meet her at Exagorà House and take her home. She hung up the call before he had a chance to ask any other questions, but he had saved up a string of them by the time he arrived.

"Are you just gonna stuff your face the whole time and

ignore me?" Chip grumbled as his truck headed to Cameron Mountain.

"I've been getting ignored a lot lately," she said, her mouth uncharacteristically full. "Why not return the favor?"

Chip clucked his tongue. Technically, he was Ian's uncle, although that revelation was just months old. He was also the first person in Poplar Gap Kristina had met last summer. He adored her. The two had become close friends before he'd helped Ian's grandfather waylay her and trap her alone in the cabin. They laughed about it now, but man, oh man, had she been furious at the time! This was the first time since then Chip had seen her this angry. As thankful as he was it wasn't directed at him, he hated to see her unhappy.

"Kristina," he said gently. "I don't know what you're so dadblamed tangled up about, but it must have something to do with Ian, or he'd be driving you, not me. Whatever it is, you'll work it out. Ian loves you."

"Odd way to show it, carrying on with Andy Cummings. In broad daylight, too, to say nothing of being at the cabin with her." Fury had fueled her appetite; her meal was quickly devoured. Kristina wiped her hands with the napkin and packed her trash neatly inside the bag.

Chip made a noise. "I don't know anything about that, but I know Ian. And I know enough about Andy that I'd be right surprised—"

"Stay out of it, Chip," Kristina said briskly. "I'm mad, okay? And I'm realizing just how little I know about your... your *dadblamed* nephew. And the rest of the people around here."

"You know me," he said stubbornly.

"Yeah, well, I thought I knew you when you tied me to a chair, too," Kristina muttered.

The truck eased into the drive just above the cabin, and Kristina immediately hopped out. "Thanks for the ride." She slammed the truck door, yanked her suitcase out of the bed, and stormed inside. Chip sat for a few minutes wondering if he should follow her, try to talk some sense into her thick head, but decided against it.

Backing up and turning around, he headed home. In a few days, he would pick up his parents from their friends' home in Asheville. Maybe they'd have some sage wisdom to offer. "Women," he muttered under his breath. At least Blue would be happy to see him when he went home.

Kristina had finally gotten used to the fact that Ian never locked the cabin, but now, walking into the room they shared, she was overwhelmed by loneliness. She hadn't been there alone since Chip and Will had left her there, tied up for her own protection, they'd said, until Ian could return from hunting last October. True, there were bear traps all over the woods. True, she'd almost stumbled into one when she had tried to run away from Ian. The memory smarted, although the spanking he'd administered had hurt her pride much more than it had hurt her skin.

While the claw foot tub filled with steaming water, Kristina put her long hair up in a sloppy bun on top of her head. Her muscles ached. She needed a long hot bath and a glass of wine. She wondered how long it would be before Ian slunk home with his tail between his legs.

After Kristina's grand exit, Ian and Andy were silent for a few moments, but Andy was soon chattering again. "I've seen photos of Disney World, of course. It looks fucking incredible. I'm Facebook friends with a few artists who work there, and I pick their brains occasionally. They've been very encouraging."

Ian nodded, fuming inside at the spectacle of herself Kristina had made. None of that was Andy's fault, however.

"You're a talented artist yourself. Do you ever think about going to an art school?"

Andy made a face. "No time soon. I wouldn't get in, anyway." She stopped eating to state the obvious, punctuated by jabbing her fork in his direction. "Your girlfriend is royally pissed. What did you do?"

Ian blew out a long breath. "For starters, I cut off a phone call with her when you came to the cabin. I forgot to call her back. Then when she asked what we'd talked about. I wouldn't tell her." In answer to the questioning look on her face, he explained, "You spoke to me in confidence. I couldn't share your story with anyone, not even Kristina, without asking you first."

Andy gave him a thumbs up. "I like that. Now that I know how talking about stuff helps, maybe I'll tell her myself. And tell her how much you've helped me the last few days." Suddenly, her eyes widened. "You mean she was jealous? That woman's fucking gorgeous!" She grinned and shook her head. "Jealous of *me*. Maybe there's hope yet."

Kristina had just finished shaving her legs when she heard the kitchen door slam. In a matter of seconds, Ian stood in the doorway of the bathroom. His face was ruddier than usual, his eyes colder. Every muscle was tense. Just by looking at him, she could tell he had spent the entire drive from Humphrey repeating their conversations from the last few days. *Focusing on every bitchy thing I've said.*

She had missed his touches, his kisses, their lovemaking. Before that awful interrupted phone call, all she would have had on her mind tonight was savoring him slowly. The man standing in the bathroom doorway now was not a man who would be touching her gently any time soon; that much was evident.

Stubbornly, she closed her eyes and rested her head back on the edge of the tub, saying nothing.

"Well?" Ian said with a hint of a snarl.

Kristina opened her eyes and looked at him blankly. "Well, what?"

"You embarrassed me, and you embarrassed yourself. I think an apology is in order."

Feelings flooded Kristina's mind from the past. Her date for the frat party had said essentially the same thing, making her feel ashamed, like she had been at fault. For many hurtful months, she had been convinced that she'd had too much to drink and ended up in bed with some random guy, when in reality, she'd been drugged and raped. And now the man she thought was the love of her life was ashamed of her? The pain was unbearable. If she tried to speak, she knew she'd break down. Instead, she closed her eyes again and turned her face to the wall so he wouldn't see how deeply his words had cut.

Ian roughly pulled her up from the water and threw her over his shoulder, carrying her into their room. Just as he had done when she tried to run away in October, he laid her across his lap and spanked her over and over. *Smack!* It stung even more because of her wet skin. *Smack! Smack!*

In shock, Kristina cried out for him to stop, squirming and scratching at his pants leg to make him stop, but he continued without mercy. Finally, when she thought it would never end, he laid a hand on her bare bottom with a sense of finality.

Without a word, Ian laid her on the bed and left the room, returning with a towel. As she wrapped it around herself and took down her hair, she heard him open the front door and let the screen door close behind him. Kristina sat on the edge of the bed, tears streaming down her face. *How could he do this to me again? What kind of man strikes a woman in anger? I'll leave. I'll leave tonight and never come back.*

You tried to leave that time, too. She thought back to that first day on the mountain. She had waited until he was busy before running out the front door into the swirling snow, quickly putting on her coat, heading for the dense woods. He'd yelled at her to stop then yanked her back hard, just as she was about to step into a steel trap. After spanking her like a disobedient child, he had prepared a meal for her, held out her chair for her. The next night, they had fallen in love.

He had been afraid she would get hurt. Afraid, not angry. Was it the same now? What was he afraid of? Getting caught with Andy? *Losing you, you idiot,* a voice spoke deep inside.

Silently, Kristina walked to the screen door. Ian sat on the edge of the porch with his head and arms draped over his knees. His shoulders were shaking. Under different circumstances, she might think he was laughing. Instead, her heart broke. This strong, noble man, *her* man, was weeping.

9

New Beginnings

The screen door creaked as Kristina opened it, but Ian did not look up. She sat down on the porch beside him and leaned her head against his arm. "I have been foolish, haven't I?"

Ian nodded, his head still hidden. When he raised his head, Kristina smiled sadly and wiped the tears from his cheeks.

"I was so afraid I'd lost you," he said huskily. "I lashed out in anger, but then the fear took over." Ian took her face in both hands and kissed her passionately. "Have I? Lost you?"

Kristina shook her head. "I was jealous and also afraid. We just met, and now we're living together, planning a wedding. I was afraid we'd moved too quickly, that you weren't the man I fell in love with. Andy is so..." She sighed. "I don't know. Young. Beautiful. Talented—"

"Bald?"

They burst out laughing and embraced. Kristina pushed him away slightly. "Seriously, though. What in the hell were you thinking? What did you think *I* would think, the two of you together here. All lovey-dovey at lunch." She punched his chest without force. "I thought you were smarter than that."

Ian nodded and pulled her close again. "Fair warning—you're going to feel bad about getting mad at Andy when I tell you this, but she did say it would be okay." One hand idly played with Kristina's hair as he spoke. "I think she'll tell you herself one day, too." Ian quietly told her about finding the paper in the file, the trauma Andy had written on it, how Andy had driven to the cabin feeling lost and unsure of herself, needing to talk to a man who would be honest with her.

"She's lonely, Kristina. So lonely, but she remembers how special that horrible man made her feel. It was all a lie, though, so she thought she must not be special at all, that *no* man would think she's special. She couldn't talk to her father. Her brothers have their own lives and issues. Helen couldn't give her a man's perspective." Ian looked up at the darkening sky. "I want to help people as a social worker, and this young woman dropped in out of nowhere needing help. I think we can *both* help her if you're willing."

Kristina nodded. "Of course. Fourteen." She shivered at the thought, suddenly aware that she was still naked under the towel as the temperature dropped. "I had such a difficult time with what happened to me, but I was *drugged*. I didn't know what was happening in the moment, which was a mercy of sorts. And I wasn't *fourteen*! Bless her heart."

Ian rubbed her arm briskly. "I think I need to get you inside." He helped her up but couldn't let another opportunity to embrace her pass.

Kristina looked up at him with unmistakable desire in her eyes. "I have a better idea. I think you need to get *you* inside. Of me."

Pete thought he was coming home quietly, but Andy met him at the back door, holding out a cold beer. "Out kind of late, aren't you, Daddy?" she teased. "Again?"

Sheepishly, Pete took the beer and kissed his daughter on top of her head as he passed her. "You could've joined us for supper, you know." He had eaten with Marilda and Jeffrey, staying for a few hours after Jeffrey had said goodnight.

Andy went to the refrigerator and pulled out another beer for herself. "Having Jeffrey there's bad enough. Didn't want to cramp your style."

Pete laughed softly and sat down in his favorite chair. Shaking his head, he said, "I'm still blown away by all this. I never thought." He frowned as he took a swig and settled back into the chair.

Andy went to the sofa and sat crisscross on it. "I'm happy for you, Daddy. I've never seen you like this. Mama Wilson, either. It's like, I don't know, a fucking miracle or something."

Pete shook his head. "It's something, all right. The logistics of it, we haven't figured out just yet but——"

"The mechanics work okay?" Andy laughed heartily. She couldn't picture it, thank heavens, but she hoped that even at their advanced age, they had no trouble in that particular department. From the blush on her father's cheeks, she was guessing she had nothing to worry about. "So. Have you talked?"

"Of course, we've talked."

"About the future."

Pete scowled good-naturedly. "You're getting ahead of yourself, bossy britches. That's none of your dadblamed business."

Andy held up her bottle of beer in salute. "I disagree. As the woman of the house since I was four fucking years old, I think it's very much my business."

"That mouth of yours is going to get you into trouble one

of these days," her father said lightly. "Say, have you heard anything from that fellow coming to interview you? Sounds kind of far-fetched to me. You think he'll really show up?"

Andy shrugged. "Maybe. I'm working at the shop tomorrow. I've got that engine almost rebuilt for Sam, and Jeb's got baseball practice after school now that spring break's over. He did okay while you were sick. When he wasn't mooning over Lucy in the store." She rolled her eyes. "I guess your and Mama Wilson's aren't the only birds and bees getting some action this spring."

10

Reese Comes to Town

Reese Maverick loved to drive. Today, he had both the perfect weather for it and, in his opinion, the perfect car. When his father had passed away, he had left Reese his prized 1967 Austin-Healey3000 BJ8 Mk III with the stipulation that he never sell it. Valued, apparently, in the neighborhood of $50,000, Reese had been tempted a few times to let the convertible go, but he respected his father's wishes too much to do so.

It made him feel closer to his father and to his roots, to drive the car. He wished he had cherished both sooner. At some point, he had become convinced that his family was unsophisticated. He had pushed them away, not overtly but by gradual neglect. And now they were gone. He missed his parents and the extended family that had been so important when he was younger. Geographic distance had been an enemy, but nothing like his own arrogance.

Sell this car? Never. As a younger, less mature man, Reese had seen the car as his father's one redeeming value. Now he knew better, but driving the car still helped his self-esteem. He'd feasted on plenty of soup for dinner during college when selling the car would have made his life more comfortable, but last wishes were not to be taken lightly. The car was painted a brilliant pearlized cobalt blue and had a black interior. In his youth, his father had attached a custom front bumper in wood, carved with his initials, but the original bumper was in storage should he ever become desperate enough to sell.

The car was, in fact, responsible for Reese's engagement. Camille Bentley, of the New York City Bentleys, had been attracted to the car before she was attracted to its driver. She'd seen it parked while visiting a friend after her classes at City College of New York and been so impressed, she had hung around until its owner showed up. Although her family had no connection to Bentley cars, she seldom volunteered that information unless pressured to do so.

Camille Bentley, *uber* sophisticated, was now Reese's fiancée. That the engagement had been her idea before it was his, was obvious to everyone. Cammie, as she liked to be called, was used to getting her way. As Reese reveled in the hairpin turns taking him into Humphrey, North Carolina, he decided there would be plenty of time and plenty of ways for him to make this weekend up to her. He'd never been asked to go on the road for a writing assignment, and he had made his boss' request priority.

"I'm not as important as your job, is that it?" Cammie had asked frostily.

Reese had used every ounce of the old Maverick charm to calm her down. He was *fairly* sure he loved her. She was Someone—good family, sizable trust fund, amazing connections. His plan, not that he would have recognized it as a plan, had been to take the first decent job he found after graduating with a major in computer science and a minor in journalism, work a few years, marry Cammie and then leverage one of those amazing connections into a career.

He hadn't counted on a few key factors, however.

Cammie was difficult. He also discovered that he had not only talent for writing and photography, but also passion. Instead of working in a glass-fronted skyscraper one day, he knew he would be happier working his way up from reporter to editor. Maybe publisher one day, when he'd done all the nuts and bolts work he wanted, finally ready for something in management. Or not. Maybe he would write the Great American Novel one day. But business? Maybe that was Cammie's dream for him, but not his.

Today, Reese breathed in the scent of the mountains, mentally describing it for the article he would compose. There was a distinctive metallic smell mixed in which he wondered about, glancing at the gauges. Nothing was amiss there, so he put it out of his mind. Hopefully Worth had been right to trust his wife's instincts about this Andy person, but if not, he'd find an even better story. Everyone has a story to tell, he often said, if you just ask the right questions and enough of them.

He didn't have a lot of information to go on, but he had let a very perky young woman know by phone of his imminent arrival. If this Andy person was out of town, he would wait. Worth had given him *carte blanche*, assuring him that he could either commute from the nearest city of Asheville or find a place to stay in Humphrey, whichever he preferred.

Cammie had been, as expected, livid at the change in plans, but that was nothing new. He was sometimes surprised to find they were still engaged at all. She'd been disappointed when he took an entry-level position at the magazine but brushed it off as a temporary situation. "I'll have you back in the Big Apple before you know it," she'd said smugly.

A baseball cap kept Reese's hair from blowing in his eyes as the breeze whipped through the convertible. He saw a sign for Humphrey and smiled. A respite from Cammie only added to the trip's appeal, but this wasn't something he would ever say aloud. He'd warned her that his cell signal would probably be weak. He'd be in touch when he could, but she shouldn't plan on regular calls.

Pete's Place came into view. The Andy person may or may not be working, but perhaps the perky girl on the phone could point him in the right direction. Reese decided to get gas first. He pulled up to one of the two pumps, noted that he'd have to go inside the store to pay, and filled up the car. As he slid the nozzle back into its spot, a voice behind him made him turn.

"Nice Mark III. Is that the original upholstery?"

Reese turned to find a woman in overalls, t-shirt, and a baseball cap watching him. She appeared to be bald under the cap. "Yes, it is," he said, extending a hand to greet her. "Reese Maverick. You must be Andy. Nice to meet you."

Andy wiped her hands on her overalls and shook his hand. "Andy Cummings. You're from the magazine?" She dropped her hand and walked slowly around the car, admiring the details. "You spoke with Lucy. What exactly did you have in mind?"

She's direct, I'll give her that. "You met Jessica Vincent. Apparently, you made quite an impression on her, fixing her car—"

Andy rolled her eyes and snickered. "It was the battery. It's not like I had to take apart her fucking engine or anything. I'll show you the shop."

"Should I move my car first?" he asked, intrigued by her language.

"Nah. Slow day." She put her hand on the hood and pulled it off quickly. "On second thought, maybe you should. The hood's hotter than it should be. Have you seen any steam? Smelled anything different?"

When he told her about the metallic smell, she nodded. "There's a space to pull it in—today's been slow." She made a little face, suddenly showing off dimples in what Reese considered a delightful way. "Not that every day isn't slow around here. Here's where we work our mechanical magic," Andy said, sweeping her arm. "That's Jeb over there changing the tire." A lanky redhead with freckles waved from his crouched position. "Do you do all your own work? On the Mark III, I mean."

Reese laughed. "Hardly. I inherited it from my father. He was the car buff. He wouldn't let me so much as add oil to it. I'll drive it in."

Andy nodded her head. "We'll let her cool down while we talk, then I'll take a look. We had a Miata in last year, but I've never worked on an Austin-Healey. Such pretty lines."

I wonder if yours are, Reese mused as he followed Andy around the shop. It was anybody's guess what Andy's shape was under the baggy overalls and t-shirt. From her silhouette, he couldn't tell whether or not she was wearing a bra, but he'd bet money that if she was, it wasn't lace. Briefly, he thought of Cammie's expensive lingerie and marveled that he didn't feel guiltier as he continued to watch Andy's bottom.

At some point, Andy removed her grease-splotched baseball cap. This had a two-fold effect. The shock of the shaved scalp was startling to Reese, but without the cap's bill in view, he saw that her eyes were equally startling, wide, full-lashed, expressive. *This is going to be a more interesting interview than I'd thought.*

"I suppose you want to see the mural? Jessica liked it. There are more at Exagorà House, but I'd have to make sure someone is there first. And I guess you want to talk to the woman with cancer?" Andy walked toward the waiting area now, modest in size and amenities, but splendid with the color and detail of her artwork.

Reese was not particularly "artsy" but he knew quality when he saw it. Andy's work was breathtaking. "Where did you study?" he asked, peering at first one wall more closely, then another.

Andy made a face. "I didn't." She gave a little bow. "Well, I *am* a proud graduate of Humphrey K-12, home of the Cardinals." She put the cap back on and pointed. Sure enough, under years of shop soil, there was a once-bright cardinal on the front.

Lucy walked in from the store with a bottle of soda. "Taking this to Jeb." She smiled first at Andy, then more shyly at Reese, keeping her usual gum popping to a minimum. "Are you the guy from the magazine?"

Reese nodded. "You must be Lucy."

Andy seemed to enjoy the girl's obvious attraction to him. "Tell Jeb Ralph's wife'll bring him to get his car as soon as it's ready. Since you're going that way."

"Jeb? Oh. Right." She gave Reese a little wave as she sashayed past to the shop.

There was a brief moment of silence as Andy watched Reese watch Lucy exit. "She's a trip, that one. Good in the store, though. Working a bit too hard to get out of Humphrey, but that's fairly common."

Reese crossed his arms. "You didn't get out. Did you want to?"

Andy gestured for him to sit in one of the two chairs; she took the other. "Are we doing this now?"

Reese pulled out a little recorder from his shirt pocket. "We can start. I like to take written notes, but this will get me started." He turned the device on. "How about you begin with your childhood?"

After talking for several hours—the time flew—Andy took Reese back into the shop. It was empty by then, and his car's engine had cooled down. She explained the basics of car care as she checked everything. "You can save a lot of money doing this yourself, and you'd have fun doing it," she told him. She stood up. "Your radiator needs water. And look here. The temperature gauge isn't working. You were running hot and didn't know it. Good thing this was as far as you were going, or the engine could have seized. Then you really *would* have been fucked."

He'd never had a woman show this kind of interest in anything he loved, or drop F bombs, for that matter. He was enjoying it. Andy was knowledgeable and a good communicator. She talked him through some basic maintenance procedures; when he did something incorrectly, she patiently explained a better way. *So different from Cammie.*

When Andy suggested Reese meet Marilda and Jeffrey next, he was surprised at how much time they'd spent together. It was close to five o'clock. *What an interesting woman,* he found himself thinking often. She appeared to have no idea how beautiful she was. Her face was beautiful, at least. Under all the grime and grit and overalls, it was difficult to guess what one might find. *I think I'd enjoy getting more insight into that topic.*

Although his questions were designed to dig deeper into her own life, she managed to bring others in, describing townspeople and events with clarity, confidence, and colorful language. The first few times she'd sprinkled "fucking" into her sentences, he'd been taken aback, but he soon saw that it was habitual, not thrown in for shock value. Her baldness already had that covered anyway.

Now he followed her truck in his car, turning his head this way and that to look at picturesque buildings, homes and flowering bushes. There were no indications that this was a wealthy community, but it was obviously one whose citizens loved it. Humphrey was clean and neat, the houses well-kept though modest.

Andy's truck pulled over to a sidewalk curb. She waved him on, directing him into a gravel driveway. "I'm pretty sure you can stay here if you want to. Mama Wilson used to take in boarders, and she still keeps a guest room open in case. When I mentioned it, she was agreeable. Unless you had other plans?"

Reese popped the trunk and pulled out a small leather duffel bag. "This'll be great. I take it you and the Wilsons are close."

They walked to the front porch, where Andy tapped on the screen door then opened it. "Forever. Jeffrey and I are almost the same age, and Mama Wilson's been good to me, haven't you?" Andy hugged the woman who entered the room with a tall, long-haired young man.

Reese wondered briefly if this fellow and Andy were a couple but quickly decided against it. There was none of that vibe in the room. They were more like a brother and sister. He might be wrong; he rather *hoped* he was wrong, but he had a sneaking suspicion that Andy Cummings was gay. Her vocabulary, look, clothes, occupation. He didn't want to make an assumption, but if he was being honest with himself, his own pride was a factor. He was used to women behaving more like Lucy had around him. Andy showed no evidence of feminine wiles or interest in him. *Darn it.*

Marilda Wilson introduced herself and her son to Reese before offering some iced tea, and then they sat—Marilda and Jeffrey on the couch, Reese in the wing back, and Andy in a wooden rocker.

"She won't let me sit on fabric when I've been working," she explained.

This time, Reese had his notebook. For the next few hours, he asked Marilda and Jeffrey questions about Andy, about the town, the chemo. Reese had spent so much time with Cammie and her crowd in the last few months, he found it surprisingly refreshing to talk with people who were so genuine, so forthright. His parents would have called them "good people."

Finally, Marilda glanced at her watch. "Pete asked us to

meet him at your house for supper, Andy." She smiled at Reese. "Pete is Andy's father, of course, the owner of Pete's Place. We are, well, we went to school together and have known each other since grade school."

Jeffrey had added a lot to the interview, surprising and impressing Reese with his ability to remember details and express himself so well. The young man gave a little smile now. "Mr. Pete is sweet on Mama. Did you know that?"

Reese shook his head then nodded. "I can see why."

"Mama Wilson, you're blushing!" Andy said with a laugh. "You'll have to come back when her hair grows back out. She's got beautiful auburn hair. Well, you do! Show him a photo, Jeffrey. Where's the one from my graduation?"

Jeffrey took a small framed photo from its place of honor on a marble-topped table and handed it to Reese. The Wilsons flanked Andy as she smiled at the camera. In the red cap and gown, it was still impossible to tell her shape. *Why so curious about that, Mav?* "Very nice," he murmured.

He glanced back and forth from the photo to the women in the room. Marilda Wilson was attractive with a blue scarf wrapped around her head, perhaps on the thin side, but she was a knock-out in the photo, with shoulder-length, curly auburn hair and ten more pounds on her frame. Andy didn't look all that different, however. However long her hair had been, in the photo, it was pulled back tightly into an unseen ponytail.

Jeffrey put the frame back in its place and announced that they were grilling hamburgers and hot dogs. "That's my favorite. What's your favorite food?"

"Anything that I don't have to cook myself," Reese quipped. "My fiancée is the same way. Ask her what she likes to make for dinner, and she'll say, 'a reservation.'"

Marilda laughed softly. "Humphrey's not fancy enough for that kind of restaurant, I'm afraid. Andy should show you around Asheville, though, if you've got time. That's where we go when we want to spend too much money. You're from the city, but Asheville's still in the mountains, different from what you're used to, I imagine. Andy's brother lives there, too."

Reese suddenly felt sad and alone. Humphrey was a delightful place and the mountains were beautiful. He knew enough about Asheville to know he'd love it. A tour with Andy would be pleasant, probably, but he enjoyed seeing new places with someone he could share the experience with on a deeper level, someone special. Someone he loved. He doubted if the mountains would be Cammie's cup of tea, though. "That would be great if it works out."

It was close to midnight when Reese stretched out in the four-poster bed under a colorful handmade quilt. The bedroom window was open, and he took a deep, satisfying breath of cool night air. Unlike in the city, there were no noises outside, save an occasional barking dog or the rustle of leaves from the big oak tree in the Wilson's side yard. Supper at the Cummings' house had been both informative and delicious. He'd forgotten how good a juicy hamburger and almost-burnt hot dog tasted when eaten outside on a picnic table in someone's backyard. Jeffrey had helped Pete cook, while Marilda made it a point to nuzzle up to Pete from time to time and exchange soft conversations with him.

Romance at their age. Andy seemed happy about it, too, as did Jeffrey. Added to that aspect, was a strong sense of family. Reese stared at the ceiling. Family. He had none to speak of. He missed the feeling of connection he'd enjoyed as a boy. He and Cammie, though engaged, had never once talked about children. Her friends didn't have children. Her relatives all seemed to have nannies and *au pairs*. It dawned on him that he hadn't been to a family gathering with Cammie that had even come close to the intimacy and sincerity of tonight's meal. He'd have to do something about that. Drifting off to sleep, he wondered if Cammie had ever eaten a grilled hot dog in her life.

Across town, Andy also stared at a ceiling from a four poster bed. Reese Maverick was certainly easy on the eyes. Professionally distant, or maybe that was just the way he was. Also engaged. A city boy. They had very little in common, nor was she hoping to find anything, now that they had spent time together. He would interview her, interfere with her daily routine for a few days, and then he'd be gone.

At some point, she'd find a magazine in the mailbox and read what he'd written, perhaps understand what he had seen when he looked at her—a bald, crude mechanic? Misunderstood artist? Country hick? She got the distinct idea that whatever he wrote about her, he would be kind. Kind. She was a little tired of men being kind but nothing beyond. *Fuck that.*

She wondered what it would feel like to be sought after again, to be desired, to be touched. She loved seeing her father with Mama Wilson. Andy had been so young when her mother left, she'd never seen Pete like this, in love, an inner fire burning again after the embers had almost gone completely out. They were intimate; she was sure of it.

At the thought, Andy's hand traced the outline of her breasts and stomach, reaching between her legs. She turned over in bed and began rocking noiselessly as her fingers found the best spots for gentle pressure. If she was destined to be alone for the rest of her life, damn it, she wasn't going to be without pleasure. Even as a young girl, she'd been able to do what she always thought of as "making her bottom giggle." As the waves of excitement grew, Andy closed her eyes.

She was surprised to see, as if in her truck's rearview mirror, a vision of Reese Maverick in his splendid blue Austin-Healey. Following her.

11

Cammie

Reese had been in Humphrey for several days, accompanying Andy to Exagorà House to meet Ian and Kristina, taking photos of Andy's unique art work there and in other locations around town. No one, including herself, seemed to know how good it was. Personally, he could see her paintings hanging in a museum in Manhattan or on the glossy pages of a coffee table art book. She was that talented.

He was so busy working on the story that he had mentally left Cammie in New York. She was, it felt, a world away; calling her hadn't crossed his mind. He had emailed and texted the usual, albeit with lessening regularity with each passing day, but he was on assignment. The lack of motivation to be in contact might have been a red flag, but Reese was wrapped up in Andy's story, which was interesting enough to blind him to almost everything else.

Reese sat cross-legged on the double bed in the Wilson's guest room, pillows stacked behind his back for support. As he tapped away on the keys of his laptop, a window popped up, indicating he had a video call from Cammie. "Hey, stranger," she cooed, her face close to the camera. "What are you doing?"

Cammie was beautiful, no question. She looked chic as always, in overpriced hairdo and perfectly applied makeup. False eyelashes fluttered over lavender eyes that always looked slightly bored. Her platinum—dyed—hair was cut in a stylish bob.

Reese lay back on the pillows and balanced the laptop on his stomach. The little window that mirrored his face showed a big grin. "I'm working, Cammie. That's what I'm doing here, working hard on the story so I can finish and get back." In truth, he didn't relish the thought of leaving the mountains, but this wasn't a vacation, after all. Worth wasn't paying him to relax, even though he had to admit, he was more relaxed in Humphrey than he had been in years.

Cammie backed up from the camera to reveal her tight, naked figure. "I thought you might need a reminder of what you gave up this weekend," she purred.

What immediately leapt to Reese's mind was not lust for his fiancée but the thought of Marilda Wilson and Jeffrey sleeping nearby. His second thought was lustful enough to cause his face to flush unexpectedly with embarrassment as his erection pressed against the underside of his computer. "You look great, Cam," he whispered.

Cammie pressed her smallish breasts together to create enticing cleavage. "Why are you whispering?" she said, making a face. "Is your hotel room nice?"

Reese held up a finger. "Shh. I'm not at a hotel. I'm staying in the guest room of one of the people I've been interviewing, a very nice woman who beat cancer, who has an autistic son. I'm whispering because it's late and this is an old house. I doubt the walls are very thick."

Cammie frowned. "So. Are you getting a story? Are you almost through? I was hoping we could play a little tonight. *You* know." She leaned in toward the camera, provocatively licking her dark red lips.

Reese bit his lip and shook his head. "Not a good idea, Cammie," he whispered. "I need to finish up a section and then hit the hay." He was instantly sorry he'd picked up on one of Jeffrey's expressions.

Cammie was incredulous. "'Hit the hay'? OMG, you sound like a hillbilly already! What have they done to you? Are they feeding you hog jowls? Serving moonshine?"

Reese smiled at the thought of his breakfasts at the Wilson's table, typically eggs, sausage, grits, and buttermilk biscuits. If he hadn't gained five pounds in the last few days, he'd be surprised. "You look delicious, Cam, but I need to finish. Maybe I can call tomorrow. No, scratch that, we're going to Asheville tomorrow."

"We?"

"Andy. The mechanic," he whispered tersely. "The bald woman who paints." *What a dismal, completely inadequate description.*

Cammie crossed her arms and pursed her lips. "At least send me some photos so I can see my competition."

Reese chuckled softly. "She's not competing for my attention or anything else. She may be gay, as a matter of fact. But I'll send photos. Love you. Thanks for the chat."

By the light of his laptop screen, Reese found his bag, removed the SD card from his camera, and inserted it into the computer. He smiled at the results, remembering the conversations and jokes that had accompanied each photo as if he were right there. That was a great one of Andy inspecting his engine, he thought. He'd mentioned it seemed to still be running hot and she had insisted on checking it out.

"The fucking hose is twisted, that's all." She'd grinned magnificently. His candid photo had caught it perfectly.

In another, Marilda and Andy sat side by side, their bald

heads touching affectionately. Worth would be pleased; he was sure of it. Without going through the many others, he selected "all" of the folder and emailed it to Cammie.

He kept scrolling down, however, spotting a photograph he hadn't taken. *Jeffrey must have picked up my camera.* Everyone else was accounted for. They'd piled into the back of Andy's truck and headed to the lake, where Andy had quietly taken him aside and told him about the minister. She didn't want it in the story, not in details, anyway, but she did want to let people know how powerful it was to bring bad memories from the darkness of their minds into the light. "It's fucking empowering," she'd said, flashing a smile.

Jeffrey must have caught that exact moment on his camera; the others were by the water's edge in the background. Andy and Reese stood close to each other under a tree. Her face was turned up to his and her smile was dazzling. The way she was standing in relation to the sun, the hint of a generous breast was outlined under the thin white t-shirt she wore under her overalls. *Wow.*

As Reese stared at the photo of himself and Andy, Cammie opened the folder in her email. She smiled, not kindly, as she scrolled through the photos. *Reese is right,* she thought. *Definitely gay. Nice eyes. Good teeth. Not a great look, though.* She kept scrolling until she found the one of Andy and Reese together at the lake. She cocked one sculpted eyebrow and drew in a breath. That was not the smile of a gay woman to a straight man. She reached for her phone. "I need a reservation from JFK to Asheville, North Carolina. Tomorrow. Of course, first class. Is there any other way to travel?

Late the next afternoon, Camille Bentley smoothed her designer jacket and looked around outside Asheville Regional

Airport, manicured hands holding the handle of an overnight bag. *Won't they be surprised?*

The drive to Asheville hadn't been hampered in the least by the fog and drizzle. Andy had wanted to drive the Austin-Healey, something she had enjoyed a few times already. Reese asked her to drive the truck instead. "You said Asheville has all kinds of cool shops. What if I buy something that won't fit in the trunk?"

As it happened, they spent the entire day touring the Biltmore Estate. Andy introduced him to her brother Clyde, who proudly showed off his work inside the Walled Garden with its 50,000 tulips, 14,000 daffodils and 1,000 hyacinths. Reese got some outstanding photos of brother and sister against a sea of color.

Reese knew that Andy was a self-taught artist, but now she revealed herself as a self-taught art history aficionado, pointing out the techniques and histories of many of the paintings hanging in the mansion. She added so many details that a nearby tour guide took her aside and asked if she'd consider applying for a job there.

Every minute with Andy made her more interesting to Reese, as if time pulled away layers and layers of...what? Protection? Assumption? Prejudice? He wished she wouldn't cuss so often and had said as much. Perhaps it was wishful thinking on his part, but she seemed to have cut back, at least slightly.

She had also grudgingly taken Kristina's advice—and the loan of some of her clothes—and ditched the overalls. Today, she wore jeans and a billowing peasant blouse, with a scarf tied around her head instead of her worn-out school cap. The jeans were a bit baggy on her and the blouse voluminous, but Reese found it to be an altogether superior look. He complimented her as soon as she picked him up at the Wilsons' house. "Nice outfit! This is the first time I've seen you without your overalls," he'd said and turned red. "I don't mean without—"

Andy had giggled. "No problem. But thank you. Kristina and Ian have been after me to, I don't know, get out of my rut? After the whole minister fuck-up I told you about, they think I subconsciously tried to hide the fact that I'm a girl. A defense mechanism, like when I was fourteen, I thought being a girl drew him to me, so I covered it up." She had brushed it aside as she settled in behind the wheel of the truck. "I think they're enjoying psychoanalyzing me almost as much as you're enjoying interviewing me."

They had spent most of the day touring the mansion and grounds. "Where to now?" Reese asked as they walked back to the truck. "An early dinner? My treat, of course." His phone vibrated in the back pocket of his khakis. Holding it up with a shrug, he stepped away a few feet as Andy opened the truck and got in.

Andy watched him through the window as he held the phone. He was surprised by whoever it was; that was clear. He kept looking over at her, frowning, as if he was trying to talk but kept getting interrupted. His face was heavy as he got back into the truck. "Change of plan. Can you drive to the airport?"

Andy offered to let Reese drive, but Cammie would have none of it. Cammie sat in the middle, so close to Reese that he was practically crammed against the door. She made a big deal of the fact that this was her first ride in a truck, brushing the seat with her hand before sliding into place.

"The seat's only really dirty where I sit on it after work," Andy had commented flatly. "Good thing we didn't bring your car, Reese, or we'd have had to tie Camille here onto the fucking hood."

Cammie whined the whole way to the restaurant Reese had looked up on his phone, one he felt would be up to her standards. The airport had been crowded, the attendants rude. At the restaurant, she continued. The decor was abysmal, the service was subpar. The food, even she had to admit, was delicious. She made it a point to keep a hand on Reese's leg, suggestively wriggling her chair closer.

To Andy, it was obvious that Camille Bentley was staking out her territory, which she found surprisingly enjoyable. *I must look better than I thought in Kristina's clothes,* she thought. *I mean, look at her! She looks like she just stepped out of* Vogue.

It was hard to get a word in edgewise, but whenever he could, Reese drew Andy into the topic of conversation, which she both recognized and appreciated. He would ask about a painting they had seen at the Biltmore or comment on the amazing landscaping Clyde was partly responsible for. "How often do you get to see his family?" he asked.

Before she could answer, Cammie interrupted. "Mother keeps badgering me about when you're coming to the city again. Soon, I hope. She wants us to start picking out china, setting up our registries."

Andy raised her eyebrows slightly. Reese had told her that he and Cammie hadn't set a date. *This is kind of fun,* she thought. *He's appalled by her behavior, but he doesn't stop her. He's so used to taking orders from her, he can't help himself.* Her respect for Reese, steadily building the more she was around him, slipped with each passing hour. By the time the threesome returned to Humphrey, Andy could hardly wait to be away from him.

Compared to the other men she admired so much—Ian, her father, Chip—Reese suddenly seemed to still be a boy pretending to be a man. Not that she'd been interested in Reese Maverick that way, but she dreamed of a man, not a boy to push around. After the interviews ended, her life could get back to normal, without complications from either Reese or his stuck-up fiancée.

At the Wilson home, Andy introduced Cammie to Mama Wilson and Jeffrey. "My bag is in the back of your truck still," Cammie said. "Would you mind getting it out for me, Andy? Which room are we staying in, Reese?"

Jeffrey laughed nervously. Marilda cleared her throat. "Reese is a guest here at Andy's request," she said. "I completely understand if he and you would like to stay elsewhere, but I have a son in high school. I'm afraid I can't allow you to spend the night here because you aren't married yet."

Andy listened with concealed amusement. Pete came home every evening, although often quite late. She thought Jeffrey would be fine with other arrangements, but she respected Mama Wilson for taking a stand in her own home. "My house, my rules," was one of her favorite lines.

The color drained from Cammie's face. Sputtering a bit, she demanded that Reese take her back to Asheville, where they could spend the night together in a proper hotel. Despite caving in to her every whim all day, though, Reese was adamant about his need to stay close for the story's sake. "I'm not leaving, Cammie. I suppose I could drive you to Asheville and find—"

"Cammie can go home with me," Andy blurted out, surprising herself. "She can sleep in the boys' old room. We're just using it for storage now, but there's still a bed there. I'll make it up for you." Something in her voice made it clear this was the only option available.

"There," said Andy as she fluffed the freshly-cased pillow. "It's not the Ritz-Carlton, but hopefully you'll be comfortable. How long will you be here?"

"I'm surprised you've heard of the Ritz-Carlton," Cammie sniffed. "Have you been to New York City? There's no place like it."

Andy was suddenly tired of this woman's incessant voice, tired of the burden of her own low expectations. She was glad Pete was already in bed when they arrived; he would no doubt have encouraged Cammie in some new vein of criticism. "I have not. Perhaps one day."

"I doubt that," Cammie muttered under her breath. She set her bag onto the bed and opened it, pulling out a flimsy black negligee. "This is one of Reese's favorites," she said smugly. "I guess it will just have to wait, thanks to that woman's uptight attitude. What a prude. And those scarves you and she wear are tacky, by the way. Hasn't anyone in this town heard of wigs?"

Andy bit her tongue. This woman, as irritating as she was, was still a guest in her father's home, even without his knowledge. She stepped closer to Cammie. "If you hear any strange noises, just ignore them. When my brother moved out a few years ago, his snake got loose, and we haven't found it yet. Fortunately, it's not poisonous. Sleep well!"

And with that, she left Cammie to her imagination and headed to her room. Before she went to sleep, though, Andy heard a muffled voice from down the hall. Opening her door quietly, she tiptoed closer and waited outside the boys' old room, the way she had done many a night, growing up. "I don't care if you're finished with the damn story on the gay girl or not," Cammie hissed. "We're going home tomorrow!"

12

Goodbyes too Soon

T he next morning, Andy tapped lightly on the bathroom door. "Cammie, breakfast's ready whenever you are." When she had explained the situation to her father earlier in the kitchen, he'd made a beeline for the shop to avoid meeting her.

By the time Cammie came to the kitchen, Andy had finished eating. She poured Cammie a cup of coffee, filling a plate from the food warming on the stove. "Here you go," she said brightly. "Did you sleep well?"

Cammie said nothing but took a long sip of coffee. "Hmm. That's good." She was dressed for travel, it appeared, with her makeup and hair done to perfection. "I couldn't possibly eat all that animal fat. Have to watch my weight for the wedding, you know." She smiled at Andy, looking her up and down with disdain for her overalls. "Do you have a significant other?"

Andy shook her head and took Cammie's plate away without a word. She carefully spooned the food into a bag for Blue and began washing the various skillets, pans, and plates.

"I wouldn't think there were a lot of people like you around here," Cammie said.

Andy didn't turn around. "Like me?"

"You know. Lesbians. You can hardly spit in New York without hitting one, but here? I'm surprised. You *should* come to the city. I have several friends who are gay, men and women. I could introduce you."

Andy calmly wiped her hands on the dish towel and brought her coffee mug back to the table, where she sat down. "Cammie," she said, as if explaining some complexity to a child. "I am not fucking gay, or vice versa, for that matter. I'm not sure how you came to that conclusion, but since you brought it up, I can assure you that I like men." *They aren't wild about me, but that's none of your business, Miss New York.*

Cammie frowned. "Oh." Her eyes narrowed. "I'm taking Reese back with me, you know. He's been gone long enough. We were going to have a wonderful weekend in the city, but he came here instead. I think he's had long enough to get his story. And he showed me the photos. Plenty of those!"

Andy nodded. "I'll be glad to take you to the Wilsons', or is he picking you up? Oh. Just had a thought. Reese *drove* here. If he flies back with you, what happens to his car?" She could see the wheels turning in Cammie's mind. Would she rather stay and ride back with him, sleeping in the Cummings' storage room with a snake that may or may not exist, or would she fly back today alone, pouting all the way?

Cammie took her up on the offer of a ride to the Wilsons' house, holding her overnight bag on her lap. "When I packed, I didn't realize it really *would* be overnight," she said with a scowl.

"Hey, look," Andy said, spotting a familiar truck as they pulled up. "Chip Murphy's here." She turned to Cammie with a look of innocence. "Chip is black. Do they have blacks in Manhattan, too, or just a lot of gay people you can spit on?"

Cammie glared at her but said nothing as she got out. Chip

Murphy and Ellen Clark, the principal of the school, walked out onto the porch.

"Hey, Chip, Miz Clark." Andy waved. "Aren't you late for school?"

Ellen Clark's smile was almost as wide as her hips. "I'm taking the day off so we can pick Will and Eleanor up in Asheville and do a little shopping." She headed straight for Cammie. "Good morning! You must be the beautiful Cammie I've been hearing about. What a quick trip you made to see your sweetheart. I'm sure he appreciated it. We're going to drop you at the airport, apparently."

"What?" Camille Bentley was not happy.

Reese walked outside, carrying a cup of coffee. He gave Cammie a perfunctory hug and kiss before explaining that he was meeting Ian Cameron for lunch. "It's the only day this week he's free, and his uncle was going to Asheville anyway, so..."

"I'll just back out so you can get out of the driveway," Andy offered lightly. *I'd love to be a fly on the seat during* that *drive,* she thought. Ellen Clark was a force to be reckoned with. Humphrey's unofficial goodwill ambassador, she was likely to give Miss Camille Bentley an earful if she got the chance. Andy and her brothers had made frequent trips to her office during their school careers.

Andy watched as Chip put Cammie's luggage in the back seat of the truck cab while Cammie and Reese said their goodbyes. Andy was surprised, and more pleased than she expected, that Reese had stood his ground. She hadn't thought the story was quite finished, either.

Cammie positioned herself so she could smirk at Andy as she got a final embrace and goodbye kiss, then made a big deal out of climbing into the back seat of the truck.

As Chip's truck disappeared down the tree-shaded street, Marilda excused herself to return inside. Jeffrey had been at school for hours. Andy and Reese were alone in the front yard. "Let's stroll, shall we? We can talk on the way. Let me grab my camera," Reese said. "Be right back."

The two of them took their time walking from the neighborhood to the downtown, stopping along the way for Andy to describe events that had happened in the town's long history. She told him more about Poplar Gap, how Kristina had met Ian. He asked about Eleanor and Will, what she knew about their complicated story. For a while, they walked in silence.

"I see you're back to overalls," Reese commented. "Are they really that comfortable?"

Andy shrugged. "For work, they are. I stick tools in the pockets, never worry about messing anything up. I haven't worn much else in a long time. One of these days, I should probably go shopping, just in case."

Reese grinned. "I plan to take you out for a nice dinner when the story's done. A 'thank you' for everything. How about wearing a dress for that?" He had plenty of photos in overalls. From an aesthetic angle alone, he needed contrast and color.

"Kristina's probably got something I could wear," she agreed. Now that Cammie was no longer pulling his strings, she realized she was not looking forward to Reese leaving. He belonged in a city, certainly. Anyone could see that. In a city with Camille Bentley? That was a bigger stretch. The two did not seem to be soulmates, at any rate. "Soulmates," she murmured aloud without meaning to.

"Soulmates? Who?"

Andy let out a breath. "Oh, I was just thinking of the happy couples I know. Ian and Kristina, Chip and Miz Clark seem pretty happy together. From what I hear, Mr. Cameron and Eleanor are as close now as when they were kids. My brother and his wife, I suppose. My other brother has a new girlfriend. My father and Mama Wilson. It's nice when people find the right person, isn't it?"

Reese nodded, so she continued. "It's like when I'm working on a car, and I just know there's something I'm not seeing. If I go inside the store and get a Coke, get a little distance, you know, when I look again, I usually see it immediately. Was it that way when you met Cammie? Or did you know right away she was the one?"

Reese frowned. "Not right away."

They walked in silence until they reached Exagorà House. Ian was attaching a flier to the inside of the glass door and opened it for them to come inside. He and Andy chatted while Reese took photographs of the two of them, as well as a few more of the artwork.

"I've got to get back to the shop, guy," she said. "See you later." Andy was used to being by herself, often working late at the shop. Jeffrey was a consistent companion, but he was still in school. *For his graduation present,* she thought, *I should paint a portrait of him in his cap and gown.* Her friend had, she knew, a bright future as an ESE aide. *And what of mine? Will I ever see beyond the mountains? Will I always be alone?*

Reese thoroughly enjoyed his lunch meeting with Ian, fascinated with the history of the area and the work they'd been able to accomplish with the grant money. Even though he'd had nothing to do with serving justice to Kristina, he was pleased to know Jessica and Worth had been instrumental in the process. He enjoyed hearing the whole big snow story, meeting Kristina, Eleanor and his grandfather. Much of the nation had rigid ideas about race relations in the South. Although the story would focus on Andy, peripheral details would help flesh it out for readers.

That night, Reese bid Jeffrey and Marilda goodnight early so he could finish his assignment. If Cammie hadn't shown up, he would have likely been finished sooner, but he was glad of the day's work he might otherwise have missed. Ian obviously adored Andy, almost like a brother. Andy was fortunate to have a support system in place, a family and then extended family on top of that.

The next morning, Reese drove to Pete's Place, where Andy's legs stuck out from beneath an ancient Buick. It had been around two in the morning when he'd sent the draft and photos to Worth, but Reese was in no rush to leave. When he kicked one of Andy's feet, she rolled out on the dolly.

"Hey! What's up? You need another unflattering photo of the bald chick?"

"As a matter of fact, I do need one more photo to add to what I've already submitted. I believe you agreed to wear a dress and accompany me to dinner?"

Andy sat up, her legs bent in a most unladylike position. "Tonight? You're done then. When're you heading back?"

Reese studied the grease-stained concrete floor of the shop. "I reckon I'll mosey on up the road tomorrow morning," he teased, adopting jargon he'd overheard in Humphrey.

"Pick me up at six, then. Let's go to Francine's Diner in Poplar Gap. She'll probably have a heart attack when I walk in wearing a dress, but she's lived a good long life. Now scoot before I make you help."

Reese drove off without a plan but found himself back at the lake where Andy had told him about the minister. Staring out at the water, he heard something from behind a mass of cattails and walked to investigate. Pete sat in a webbed lawn chair with a cane pole, watching a bobber dance gently some yards out in the water.

"Pull up a spot of ground," he said easily. "I'm playing hooky from the shop. Sorry I didn't get to meet your fiancée last night. Marilda says she's a real looker."

Reese nodded and sat down on the grass beside Pete's chair. "She is at that."

The men sat in silence for several minutes. "I'm taking Andy to Francine's Diner tonight," Reese finally said. "She's wearing a dress."

Pete chuckled. "That girl. Where in the Sam Hill she got that cussing, I don't know. She didn't hear it from me or her mother, I'll have you know. Not that she got much at all from her mother." He sighed and looked down at Reese. "I had no idea I'd ever fall in love again. Wasn't looking for it. Didn't worry about it. Hooking up with Marilda after all these years, I don't think I've ever been this happy in my life. Life sure can be strange."

"Indeed, it can."

Kristina dropped a dress off on her way to school. "It's too small for me, so keep it. Here. Try these, too."

Andy held a gold hoop up to one ear. "With a scarf?"

Kristina frowned and took off Andy's cap. "No scarf. I think your bald look is stunning. Honest."

"Not for long, though. Mama Wilson's hair is finally starting to come back, so I'm going to stop shaving. Pretty soon, I'll look like a boy *with* hair," Andy said.

Kristina took Andy's face in her hands. They had become close since Kristina apologized for what Andy referred to as her "bitch fit." And closer, since Andy confided in her about the minister. There had been many late night phone calls, but every day, Andy felt a little better about her life and possibilities.

"You do not look like a boy, my friend. Reese Maverick's eyes are going to pop plumb out of his head when he sees you tonight. I'm not convinced his interest is strictly journalistic."

Andy shook her head. "He's a city boy with big plans, Kristina. Any man who's engaged to a woman like Cammie is not interested in a woman like me."

"Maybe."

Hours later, Reese pulled up to the Cummings' two-story frame and let himself in the front door with a shout of, "Hey, I'm here!" It struck him as odd that in only a short time, he felt completely at home in Humphrey and with the families he'd met. In all the while he'd been with Cammie and visited her parents' homes in the city and on Long Island, he was still stiffly greeted at the door by a butler, waited on hand and foot but never really at *home.*

"I'm ready," Andy called down.

Reese looked up the staircase and caught a glimpse of shapely legs underneath a handkerchief hem of diaphanous material. Reese was stunned at the transformation coming toward him. The bodice of Andy's dress was delectably form-fitting, showing off shapely hips, a narrow waist, and large, rounded breasts. His eyes followed the lines of the dress from the scoop neck with a tantalizing hint of cleavage upward to the now-familiar face. Instead of a scarf or hat, her head was bare, adorned with delicate gold *hoop* earrings. In his wildest imagination, he had never envisioned Andy Cummings looking *this* sexy.

When she was at his level, she spun around, sending the hem flying up to reveal even more thigh. "You take my breath away, Miss Cummings," Reese said, holding out a bent elbow. "Shall we?"

"We fucking shall," she said with a laugh then brought a hand quickly to her mouth. "Oops! I am trying to do better.

Kristina brought the dress over after school. You like? She said it was too small for her, but it's okay on me?"

"Oh yeah," he said with enthusiasm. "You look good enough to eat, as a matter of fact. Maybe we don't need the diner after all."

Andy threw her head back with a loud guffaw as they walked to the car. "You." Even though he was joking, she appreciated the effort. "May I drive?"

The road between Humphrey and Poplar Gap was a series of tight curves, which Andy took much faster than Reese would have done. "I feel like a race car driver!" she squealed. "Waa Hoo!"

Reese gripped the sides of the passenger seat and threw back his head. "Waa Hoo!"

Over a dinner of meatloaf, mashed potatoes and fried okra, Reese Maverick marveled at the woman sitting across from him. Rough around the edges, certainly, but absolutely delightful. For a change, she was the one asking questions, about his family, his job, his plans.

He even shared his regrets, pushing his parents away in his youthful zeal to, "make something of himself, whatever that meant," he added ruefully.

Only when she asked about Cammie, did he become evasive. "No, we haven't set a date." Reese changed the subject to awards, accomplishments, medals his father had gotten in the military. "I'm not going to be a reporter forever, you know. One day, maybe I'll own the magazine. A string of magazines!"

Andy frowned, buttering one of Francine's famous yeast rolls. "I'm confused. I thought you loved to write, to meet people, to help them tell their stories."

"Well, sure. Now. But it's a stepping stone. Cammie has a lot of connections. In a few years..." His voice continued to talk, but Andy stopped listening. She had been correct. This was a man who could never be happy with a woman like her. He'd said it himself—he had pushed away family he'd judged as unsophisticated. He wanted special, special recognition, special privileges, the kind of life he would be more likely to find with Camille Bentley. She was surprised at how sad this struck her.

Reese's natural inquisitiveness picked up on the shift in Andy's mood, although he didn't connect it with his words. As they walked back to the car, he offered to let her drive one last time.

"That's okay, Reese. Thank you, though."

She was quiet on the ride from Poplar Gap to Humphrey. She didn't want to tell this man goodbye. She wanted him to stay, but he wouldn't be happy there and she couldn't be happy, she knew, if he stayed because of her. Instead of asking him inside for a beer, she shook Reese Maverick's hand and patted the hood of the car. "It's been nice knowing you, city boy. Thanks for dinner."

"This is it, I guess? I'll send you the magazine as soon as it's in print." Reese surprised Andy, and himself, by pulling her into his chest for a long hug. "I'm going to miss…Humphrey."

Andy forced a smile. "Humphrey is going to miss you, too. Oh, and don't forget to get that temperature gauge replaced. Check the water from time to time before it comes, just to make sure you don't run hot again."

She watched him drive away, her heart pounding. His embrace, however chaste, had excited her to her core. *You're running a mite hot, too. Just as well he's leaving.*

13

A Surprising Turn of Events

Months after Reese Maverick's Austin-Healey headed north, life was somewhat back to normal. The magazine had come out, been mailed, read and circulated. Andy had been a town celebrity for what she liked to say was "a minute and a half" but other events quickly distracted her and her immediate circle.

When Eleanor Rigby and Will Cameron, Chip's biological parents, returned from Asheville, they'd asked all of Ellen Clark's family to join them and Ian and Kristina on the mountain for a special meal, including the Cummings and Wilsons. It had been a grand day, but before everyone went their separate ways, Will asked for everyone to gather 'round and settle down for an announcement.

"You all know Eleanor and I were in love very young. Her parents didn't approve, since she was black, and I am white. We were ahead of our time, in that respect, I suppose. She was torn away from me. I didn't know she was carrying my child at the time, our own Chip. She wasn't sure, either. As you know, he was taken at birth and raised by adoptive parents who, thank God, raised him right. And he came back to Poplar Gap as if by divine providence, so that one day, he'd be reunited with us."

Will's voice was heavy with emotion. "Thanks to some good folks who helped us, we learned the truth. But we haven't been the family we dreamed of when we were teenagers. We brought you together today to tell you that now we are. While we were in Asheville, Eleanor and I got hitched."

An uproar of cheers filled the air. Because of their age—mid-eighties—most people who would have been offended by youngsters "living in sin" had turned a blind eye to Eleanor and Will's shared home. It was obvious they loved one another, though.

"What day did you actually get married?" Ian asked loudly. "We need to know when your first anniversary will be so we can celebrate again."

Eleanor gave the date, soon after they had traveled to Asheville. "What did you do the rest of the time?" one of Ellen Clark's grown sons called.

Will grinned and gazed down at his petite wife before answering. "Don't you know what follows a wedding?" Will laughed. "The honeymoon!"

The following week, Chip popped the question to Ellen. They had skirted the issue before; he knew she was as fond of him as he was of her, but they had maintained a frustratingly chaste relationship for the last six months. She had her job to think about, he supposed, and her women's circle at church. She was fine with kissing and hugging, she'd made it clear, but that was all. Chip hoped she would be amenable to other activities once married. In his opinion, it was time.

"I love you, Ellen," Chip said after dinner one Tuesday evening. It was a rare night with just the two of them, no children or grandchildren visiting. Chip would head back to his lonely, empty house in Poplar Gap soon so she could get ready for school the next day. "I want to be with you in every way a man can be with a woman. My parents waited over fifty years to get married, but I'm not that patient."

Ellen nodded solemnly the same way, he imagined, she nodded at errant students or problem parents. She crossed her fleshy arms over that incredibly generous bosom of hers and pursed her lips. "Are you asking me to marry you so you can share my bed?"

Chip sighed. It was true; he would have been able to put up with staying single much longer if able to enjoy her more, but he no longer wanted to live alone, not even if she didn't want sex. Maybe it had been too long for her. She was no longer interested in all that foolishness of youth, he thought. But he still loved her. With a heavy heart, he nodded. "I was. But even if we never share a bed, I want you to be my wife."

Ellen wrapped her big arms around him and kissed him squarely on the mouth, long and hard, inviting him to explore her more fully with his hands than she had ever allowed. Finally, she took a slight step back and fixed him with her steely gaze. "Chip Murphy, I will be honored to be your wife. And just to let you in on a little secret," she lowered her voice, "if you leave this house one more night without making love to me, I will be highly disappointed."

Chip's jaw dropped and his eyes narrowed in disbelief. "You mean to tell me I could've had my way with you before now? Woman, you've held out on the wrong man." He pulled Ellen down over his lap—not an easy task, since she outweighed him, but he was empowered by desire.

"What in the world?" Ellen cried, clearly enjoying the moment.

"You be quiet, now, you hear? The principal's going to get a taste of her own discipline and high time." Chip reared back his right hand and swatted her firmly on her ample behind. *Smack! Smack!*

Ellen's deep giggle was coquettish. "I don't know, Chip Murphy. I think I spanked my young'uns harder than *that*. Are you sure you know what you're doing?"

Chip chuckled. "I'm just warming up, Miss Prim and Proper. Miss String Me Along. All these months and you just waiting for me to do something about it," he muttered with a grin. *Smack! Smack! Smack!*

He stopped, caressing Ellen's bottom, reaching under her skirt to trace along her ample curves to the hot place between her legs. When she let out a little groan of pleasure, he murmured, "Do you want more, or have you learned your lesson?" he asked.

Released from his grip, Ellen stood and faced him, unbuttoning her blouse. It was his first glimpse of the enormous breasts that threatened to spill out of the matronly white bra containing them. "Oh, honey," she said, arching an eyebrow. "I definitely want more. I want a *lot* more. And I think you're just the man to give it to me."

Twenty minutes later, from the bedroom she had kept sacrosanct for many years, Ellen Clark let out a scream of ecstasy that was so loud, Chip wouldn't have been surprised if the whole town could hear her.

He didn't care one bit.

Andy put the finishing touches on a new radiator installation, singing along with Jeffrey to the portable radio on a shelf. Her hair had grown out about an inch, thicker than she had feared and curlier. The weight of her long hair had led her to believe her hair to be wavy but fairly straight. Instead, a soft halo of dark brown curls framed her face. Comments ranged from "cute" to "adorable"—two adjectives she'd never had much use for, but she had to admit it was preferable to having her bald head stared at. And the upkeep was considerably less.

Jeffrey had stopped by after school, more excited as each day passed because he would finally graduate. As they sang and chatted, he flipped through one of the car magazines that seemed to multiply every month.

"Done!" Andy announced. She wiped her hands on a shop towel hanging from a pocket. "I'm ready to get something to eat, how about you?"

Jeffrey didn't hear her at first, intently reading something in the magazine.

Andy threw the towel at him, hitting him in the face.

"Hey!" he yelled. "Wait. I'm reading about something you should do." He handed the open magazine to her.

"'American Automotive announces its biennial contest for new designers,'" Andy read aloud, skipping through type to get to the details. "'Any media permitted. $5000 first place cash prize. Entries much be postmarked by June 15.'" Andy flipped the magazine over to look at the cover. "Jeffrey! This magazine is old. If I entered the contest, I'd have, like, two weeks!. Everyone else will have had two *years*!'"

Jeffrey laughed and stuck his hands under his armpits and waved his elbows up and down as he sat perched on the stool. "Brokkk, brokk-brokk, brokk. Andy is a chicken. Andy is a chicken!"

This time, Andy rolled the magazine into a tight tube and hit him with that. "I'm not chicken; I just don't have time. This is a big deal. Maybe I'll enter the next one, then I'll have two whole years to get ready."

"Brokk, brokk," he continued then jumped off the stool. "Let's go home."

More and more often, they found Pete and Marilda at the Wilson house together, but today, there was a strange car in the driveway, parked beside Pete's truck. Jeffrey noted the license plate with a frown. "I think this car belongs to my father."

Andy grabbed his hand to walk with him. "How long has it been since you've seen him?" she asked softly, hurting for her friend. She understood the feeling of abandonment all too well.

"Seven years ago, on April 28th. He was wearing a blue plaid shirt and brown pants and said I would be getting taller. I did," Jeffrey said. He smiled at Andy. "Mama says I am taller than he is, and that I am better looking."

Together, the friends walked inside. Pete and Marilda were on the couch.

Jeffrey's father sat in the wing back, but he stood as they entered. His smile was genuine; he gave his son an awkward hug, which was not returned but tolerated. "I see you're still wearing your hair long," Jeff, Sr. said. "And is this Andy? My goodness, the last time I saw you, you were just a tiny thing. Time sure flies."

Pete cleared his throat. "Sit down, both of you. This concerns you too." He looked at Marilda and smiled. "I asked Marilda to marry me a few weeks ago. She said no."

Andy was confused. "You seem pretty happy about it. What's going on?"

"I wanted to say yes, Andy. No question about *that*. But I needed to take care of something first," Marilda said. "You see." She paused until Pete nodded for her to go on. "I couldn't say yes because I was already married."

"What the fuck?"

Pete was stern. "That's no way to talk to your——"

Andy was furious, pacing around the parlor, fighting the urge to pick up one of Mama Wilson's prized figurines and throw it across the room.

Jeffrey sat, silent and bewildered.

"That's no way to talk to my *what?* All this time, she's still been married to this fucking *loser.* And Jeffrey—"

Jeff interrupted, holding up a hand. "It's not her fault, Andy. I left her, remember? I left her and my son. I was scared. But I wanted to do right by them. I sent money—"

Andy pulled the man out of the chair and screamed into his face, lashing out with all the hurt she'd bottled up toward her mother and on Jeffrey's behalf. "He didn't need your fucking money! He needed a father!" She pushed him back into the chair.

It was Jeffrey who calmed her down, as he had calmed her down many times over the years when someone at school would make fun of her, or when she was lonely for her mother. He took her by the hand and led her to the dining table to sit beside him, holding his hand. She was shaking, she was so angry, but he patted her softly on the hand, the way he patted the hands of angry children at school who were unable to process their emotions any other way.

Jeff sat with his head down, nodding sadly. "Andy's right, of course. I am so sorry, Marilda. And especially Jeffrey. I was scared. I thought it was my fault. I wanted to fix things and couldn't. I gave up on you, and I gave up on myself. I gave up on us. I wish I could take it all back. But this is something I *can* do." He pulled a paper out of his shirt pocket that looked as though it had been folded and unfolded many times.

Marilda smiled and handed him a pen, explaining to Jeffrey and Andy that she had contacted him after Pete's proposal, asking for a divorce. "I could have divorced him long ago, but I had no reason to. He could have divorced me, but he didn't. In his own way, he kept taking care of us. And now he's letting us go."

Jeff shook his head. "I'm letting *you* go, Marilda." He signed on the correct line and handed it to her, then he stood. "Jeffrey, I don't want to let you go again. You're a man now. You needed a father, and I failed you when you were a child. You don't need me now, and Pete, here, will be the one you go to for advice, no doubt. He's a good man. I know that. He always has been." Jeff walked over to the dining table and gently pulled Jeffrey's long ponytail. "I hope you can forgive me and let me be part of your life again. However much you'll let me."

Tears fell and hugs were exchanged while the five of them consumed a pitcher of iced tea. Finally, Jeff announced he thought he'd head out. "I've tentatively decided to move to Poplar Gap," he told them, "if it's okay with Jeffrey. Will Cameron has a rental house his son's going to show me. After that, may I take us all out to eat at Francine's Diner? Is it still open?"

A time was set to meet there, and Jeff made his exit. It was only after he'd gone to meet Chip that Andy drew in a surprised breath. "Jeffrey! Your father *pulled your hair*. I've never seen anyone *touch* your hair without some kind of response, and never a good one! I am amazed."

Jeffrey nodded solemnly. "I was surprised, myself. Maybe I was just waiting for *him* to do it."

Andy offhandedly mentioned the design contest to her father on her way upstairs to go to bed that night, surprised by his enthusiastic response. "Damn it, Andy, you *need* to enter! Who cares if you win? The experience will be good for you. Jeb and I can handle the shop for a few weeks. I want you to do this. You're a damn good artist—hell, you blew Reese Maverick away with your talent."

That's all that impressed him, apparently. She knew it was fool-ish, but she couldn't stop thinking about him. For all she knew, he and Cammie had set a date. They could've gotten married! *Leave it to her to find out he wanted kids and get pregnant just to make it happen*. It was an ungenerous thought, *but Camille Bentley would*, she thought, *stop at nothing to get her way*. Only that one time had she seen Reese go against her wishes. *Because of* you, she told herself.

Lying in bed, Andy decided to take her father up on his offer. She welcomed a break from the shop. She'd been going to support group meetings more often, helping at the school with art classes for Kristina's ESE students after school once a week. even drilling Ian for his final exam. She'd also done what she considered to be an obscene amount of shopping. Now that she knew what size she was in every possible part of her anatomy, she'd ordered a whole new wardrobe. On faith, Kristina told her, "You may not know when you'll need it, but you will. When it happens, you'll be ready."

I'd need clothes to go to New York, she thought drowsily, hugging a pillow to her chest. The award banquet would be in the end of June. It would be fun to go, even if she didn't win. Maybe Jeffrey would go with her. *We could stay with Cammie's family*, she thought wryly. *Or with Cammie and Reese.*

14

Graduations of Different Kinds

As soon as the pressure from Reese's interview had ended, Andy devoted what spare time she had to painting a graduation portrait of Jeffrey. Everyone loved it, of course, and it now hung in a special place of honor over Marilda's mantel. Soon, it would be Marilda and Pete's mantel. They planned to follow Will and Eleanor's lead, marrying at a justice-of-the-peace's office in Asheville after Jeffrey graduated at the end of May. He and Andy would go along for the ride, to cheer them on and to serve as witnesses, for the one day; Marilda and Pete would stay for a weekend honeymoon.

Now, Andy worked on the contest. All her life, she had loved cars, dreaming of exotic shapes and designs. But she was practical also. Having worked on so many different cars, she knew appearance was only part of a great car's design. It needed to perform as well.

Jeb was pleased he'd be getting more work. He announced to her, in confidence, that if he could save enough money that summer, he would propose to Lucy. Andy encouraged him to wait, knowing he probably would not. *Some people have to learn the hard way.* They were both far too young and immature in her opinion. *Like I'm so wise about such things.* She had spent hours and hours filling multiple drawing pads with sketches, but now she worked on the entry itself.

Her design had elements of classic designs but also whimsy. She was designing a car for a woman, really for herself. She'd considered colored pencils but had switched to acrylics. It was a strong design, a car that wouldn't break down because it was so well-built but with feminine details and lines. Never in her imagination did she think it would win, but maybe someone in the industry would notice. Maybe she'd meet someone she could reach out to in later years, after she had gotten some formal training. Or not. Every day, she grew more excited about submitting her entry and dreamed of attending the awards banquet scheduled for August first.

Andy worked so diligently that she battled resentment at "wasting" a whole day in Asheville, but family came first. Pete and Marilda's wedding went off without a hitch, and she and Jeffrey sang all the way back. "Do you want to stay at my house tonight? You've never been in the house alone, have you? Come to think of it, I haven't been alone at my house, either."

Jeffrey smirked. "Andy. We are in our twenties. We are independent and have jobs. Well, I will start my job at the school in a few months. We aren't babies." He paused. "And my father is picking me up to stay with him in Poplar Gap."

"You might have led with that," Andy said with a laugh. "That's great. I'm glad you two are getting along."

Jeffrey nodded. "He was a selfish jerk when I was little, but now he's better."

Sure enough, when Andy turned onto his street, Jeff, Sr.'s car was waiting in the driveway. She was amazed at the change in the man; not that she had known him well when he left, but from what she had heard from others, she had expected someone much rougher around the edges, less caring. *Come to think of it, if people moved away in the last few years and returned to visit, they might recognize a few changes in me too.*

Back at the house, she wandered through every room with melancholy. She could live there, alone, as long as she wanted to. Her father would move in with Marilda and Jeffrey. She could rent out a room, she supposed. If, wonder of wonders and miracle of miracles, she ever left Humphrey or met someone and stayed there forever, her father would probably sell the house, or perhaps rent it out in case one of the boys or Jeffrey wanted it in the future.

She understood why he wasn't anxious about holding onto it. This house had witnessed happy memories, but for her father, there would always be the sting of rejection attached to it. Andy smiled as she imagined the sound of future children's laughter echoing through the house she had always called home. *I'll make a damn good aunt.*

She sat in the living room in her father's favorite rocker, listening to the familiar drone of the mantel clock. She closed her eyes and listened to the quiet sounds of the house that had calmed her since childhood. Without a mother to do that important task, she had taken comfort where she could. She saw more clearly now, how her mother's absence had changed her as a child.

"Significant loss changes you," Helen had told the support group one night recently, "and you spend the rest of your life discovering who you are *now*. Many of you lost your innocence. Some of you lost a parent or sibling. Lesser losses—a job, a break-up—can be significant too. Let yourself learn from those things and not be pulled down by them, but also know that they have changed you. It's up to you whether or not the change becomes a positive one or not."

Andy realized now, that for a long time, she had let the loss of her mother, the abandonment, fester like an oozing sore. She'd clung to her father and brothers when she might have reached out more easily to Mama Wilson or her teachers or even Sylvia Sanderson. Her mother hadn't treated her as something to cherish, as special; her father and brothers hadn't known how to—not like a mother, anyway. She'd been a sitting duck for George Sanderson. *Another significant loss.*

And now she had lost Reese Maverick. It had been easy to tell him of her past, perhaps because she'd already opened up to Ian and Kristina. But there was something about Reese that went beyond his journalistic curiosity. She had felt he was truly interested in her life. *He made me feel special.* Andy frowned. She'd never thought of it like that before, not when it came to him. She had his number, although she hadn't felt compelled to use it since he left. She texted him now, that she'd like him to call if he had a chance, and headed upstairs to shower.

She'd just taken off her clothes when he called. "That was quick," she said.

"How's my favorite bald chick?" Reese asked.

"N-not too bad," she said, not wanting to go into all that. Her baldness had been a factor in bringing him there; now she was just someone with short curly hair, nothing unique. "How about yourself, now that you're a hotshot writer for a national magazine, thanks to me. Did you ever get that new gauge for the car?"

Reese chuckled and told her that yes, the car was great. "I'll have you know I even changed the oil all by myself," he said.

Andy tried to imagine where he was. It was probably too late for him to be at the office. On his way to see Cammie? Already there?

"You caught me in the car," he said. "Hang on. I'm pulling over." Pause. "I'm back. So catch me up on the Humphrey gossip."

Andy went to her room and lay on the bed. "There's a lot, actually. Jeb thinks he wants to marry Lucy, Will and Eleanor

Cameron got married, and today, so did Pete and Marilda. Chip and Ellen are testing the suspension—"

"What? In his truck? I don't understand. Translate from hick, please."

"That's not fucking hick, you idiot," Andy said, laughing. "The suspension of her *bed*. They're bumping uglies. Hanky-panky. Making whoopee if you prefer. They're also getting married one of these days, but Chip is in such a better mood, it's easy to assume why."

"That *is* a lot going on. How's Jeffrey taking all the changes?"

"Oh, that's just the tip of the iceberg. Jeffrey graduated, has a job with the school in August, and his father came back and is living in Poplar Gap! He's staying with him this weekend, as a matter of fact. Now it's your turn. What's new with you?"

"Not so much," Reese said. "But you've told me about everyone but yourself. Has the shop been busy?"

As Andy explained her contest entry to him, how she had so little time to prepare, her enthusiasm grew even more. He had been the first person from outside her little community to notice her talent, to regard her not as a girl who painted, but as an artist. It was one of the reasons he made her feel special, she realized suddenly. *He sees me with different eyes. He understands.* "I'm not going to win, obviously, but it's been a blast working on it. The biggest challenge I've had in a while. And," she said dramatically, "I bought a whole new wardrobe, so I won't stand out like a sore thumb when I go to New York for the awards banquet."

At the mention of the city, she thought Reese drew in a breath, but she wasn't sure. He didn't respond. *Surely, New York City is big enough to hold both me and his fucking fiancée.*

When Reese finally spoke, his voice was tired. "I'm sorry, Andy, but I need to go. It was great talking to you. Good luck with the contest!" *Click.*

Andy shrugged as she stared at the ceiling. *It was good to hear his voice, anyway.* Deep down, she had hoped to sense a spark of something different, something...special...between them. It just wasn't there. *Good to know.* She walked naked to the bathroom before she realized that *that* was a first. Living with her father and brothers, it would have never entered her mind to traipse down the hall without her clothes on. *Maybe going solo won't be so bad after all.*

Andy stood at the tiny post office counter with her contest entry packaged within an inch of its life. She and Jeffrey had pored over the instructions so as not to get the tiniest detail wrong and risk disqualification. She didn't expect to win, but she "fucking sure didn't want to be rejected outright," she'd told him.

"I thought you were not cussing anymore," Jeffrey had said, handing her more packing tape.

"I never said 'anymore.' I said 'less'."

It was June 14. She watched the postal clerk, one of Ellen Clark's sons, stamp it, his meter clearly showing the date.

"The United States Post Office will take good care of this for you," he said with a smile, knowing full well what it was. The whole town was rooting for her.

"Thanks," Andy said, relieved to get it mailed but anxious to let it go. She was pleased with her work, but she hailed from Podunk County, Nowheresville. She could hear Ian and Kristina assuring her that if nothing else, she had a trip to New York planned. How great was *that*?

Andy straightened her shoulders and walked down the sidewalk, whistling as she went.

Reese sat down across from Worth and Jessica and pitched a new story as they listened intently, interrupting occasionally to clarify a detail, nodding and smiling. "What do you think?" Reese asked them finally. He'd been sitting there for a half hour—sitting most of the time, anyway. At various points, he found himself jumping up, pacing, restless in his intensity.

Jessica and Worth exchanged a look, stifling the smiles that threatened to diminish their employee's obvious sense of purpose. Worth cleared his throat. "Your pitch is approved. You can work the details out with Skip." He stood and extended his hand to Reese. "Go for it, Reese."

When Reese was safely gone and the door closed, Jessica and Worth burst out laughing.

"He has got it *bad!*" Worth took his wife in his arms, stretching his arms to reach around her. Almost full-term, he would have preferred that she rest at home, but she insisted on coming to work until the baby arrived. "Was I that intense when I was falling in love with you?"

Jessica moved her arms around his neck and looked up for a kiss. "I think you may have had him beat."

Worth's lips were tender on hers, but there was heat behind them. "Speaking of *having* someone," he murmured. "How long has it been since we gave Skip something to gossip about during office hours?"

"Too long, love," Jessica said with a giggle. "If I lean on the desk, you could come in from behind without having to navigate this enormous belly, I suppose. Want to give it a try?" She walked over to lock the door but stopped there. "Worth?"

"Yes, love? Just making some room for you on the desk," he said, stacking papers to one side.

Warm water trickled down her legs and onto the carpet. "Hold that thought," Jessica said, turning around. "And take me to the hospital please."

"Are you sure you have everything?" Kristina giggled. "Listen to me! I sound like my sister Layla, clucking like a mother hen. I'm so nervous and excited for you, I can hardly stand it!" She stood across from Andy, with a suitcase open on the bed between them.

Andy made a face. "If it's not in the suitcase now, I don't think it will fit. Why do I need so many fu...I mean, so *many* clothes?"

"Very good, Andrea," Kristina said with the air of a teacher. "You almost said 'fucking' but caught yourself. A-plus for the last, what, five minutes?" The women got the giggles.

"My first trip farther than Asheville, my first airplane ride, my first look at the big city." Andy blew out a long breath. "Do you think I'm ready for this? I mean, my hair's not bad." She turned around and then this way and that, studying her reflection in the vanity mirror. "The clothes are a vast improvement over my greasy overalls, I must agree. But..." she stopped and looked suddenly terrified as she whipped around to face her friend, "...am I ready for New York?"

Kristina walked around the four-poster bed to take her friend by the hands. "The question is," she said, holding Andy at arm's length, "is New York ready for *you*? You've come so far, just in these last few months. I'm proud of you. And I'm so very sorry—"

Andy stuck out her tongue and broke away to look in the mirror again, fingering the soft dark curls that had grown enough to tickle her neck. "Will you shut up? You've already apologized for being a bitch." She fingered her curls, remembering that she hadn't mentioned her hair to Reese the night he called. Her baldness had been part of her uniqueness for the story, after all. Out of the overalls, she didn't even resemble a mechanic any more. Now, she was just an ordinary woman.

It still shocked her that Kristina had been jealous of her. *Or Cammie*. Not that either had anything to worry about.

Andy put her hands on her hips. "Do you want anything from the Big Apple for a wedding present? I might have time to shop. I should look for something for Jessica's baby too." All reports were good—Layla called Kristina regularly and sent her photos of the happy family. Baby Lily and Jessica had come through with flying colors and Worth was so proud, he could not contain it.

On impulse, Andy pulled out the velvet box from the vanity's drawer and threw it in the suitcase before closing it a final time. Her expensive ticket and hotel room had been paid for, surprisingly, by the Exagorà Foundation. "I still can't believe you're paying for the whole trip. You didn't have to do that."

Kristina beamed. "What better way to spend the foundation's money than to send a budding young artist on her first trip to the big time? Just promise you'll come back in time for the wedding. August first. The big day! I need my bridesmaid."

Layla would be her matron-of-honor. Angela would be the flower girl. Will and Chip would stand with Ian. The excitement of Andy's trip was one thing—as soon as they'd dropped her at the airport in Asheville, though, she and Ian had a ton of details to finalize. Andy saluted. "Yes, ma'am, sir!"

Andy flew to New York in a daze, blown away by the airport, the first class cabin, and by the many hopeful glances her way from all manner of men she encountered along the way. She decided it was like something Reese had told her. 'It's always good to take people's photos when they're happy, because they usually come out well.' She couldn't hide her excitement, and it must show. She was oblivious of the attraction inspired by her curls, big eyes, and shapely figure inside the new, more flattering clothes.

Outside of baggage claim at JFK, Andy walked to the curb. A smartly uniformed attendant asked if she'd like him to hail her a taxi. "Oh hell no, mister," she said, her eyes round. "I'm from Humphrey, North Carolina. I *got* this." She set down her suitcase, licked her lips, inserted her middle and index fingers into her mouth, and blew a whistle so loud, the attendant jumped back in shock.

A cab immediately appeared at their side, popping its trunk. As the attendant stowed her suitcase away, he called out to her, "Have a pleasant stay in the Big Apple, Humphrey!"

15

A Banquet of Emotions

Kristina, having heard all the sordid details from Cammie's overnight stay, was particularly pleased to discover that American Automotive's annual meeting and contest banquet were to be held in the Central Park Ritz-Carlton's ballroom. She booked Kristina into a park view suite for five nights, explaining that she could extend the visit as long as she wanted, provided she return in plenty of time for the wedding.

Now, Andy stood in the suite in a state of awe. The king-sized bed was covered with a pristine white, goose down duvet. There was a living room with chairs, a couch, a bar. She walked around, admiring the many elegant details. The bathroom was all shiny marble. There was a vase of fresh flowers on the dresser. There was even a telescope to gaze down at Central Park. Every possible desire had been anticipated. "It's a far cry from Humphrey," Andy said aloud with a snicker, "but I reckon it'll do."

Too excited to rest, Andy changed into a more comfortable outfit of jeans, tank top, and sneakers. Grabbing her purse, sunglasses, and room key, she decided to explore. She'd always heard that New Yorkers weren't friendly, but that wasn't her experience at all. It didn't occur to her that her own openness and friendliness would make a difference. From the doorman, to the man at the newspaper stand, to the new mother sitting in the park with her baby in a carriage, Andy made friends everywhere she went. And the man at Billy's Hot Dog Cart near the park provided both an excellent dinner and tips for getting around the city.

The banquet was slated for the following night. Andy anticipated spending the next day enjoying the city, until time to get ready. After exploring the immediate area for several hours, she returned to the Ritz-Carlton, finding a packet of information on the couch, which had been delivered to her room. Formal wear was requested. There were menu choices on a little card to select and return. Entries would be displayed one hour before the banquet began at seven, and contestants were encouraged to be present.

A shiver of excitement went through Andy. Her artwork would be displayed publicly in New York. It was thrilling and also a little scary. What if people made fun of her pitiful effort? Anyone could enter, after all.

Winners were not obligated to be in attendance, and she assumed some would be unable to go to the trouble and expense of the banquet. Thanks to Exagorà, she had the pleasure of embracing the evening and the city, fully. After a long soak in the enormous jetted tub, she watched a brand new movie she'd heard good things about, enjoyed a beer from the stocked refrigerator, and went to sleep, stretching her arms and legs in all directions. It was her first time sleeping in any bed but her own, much less a king-sized, and it felt heavenly.

She woke to the ringing of her cell phone, surprised that the sun was up. *I guess I was more tired than I thought.* Ten o'clock! She'd never slept so late in her life. She fumbled for her phone and smiled as she answered. "Good morning, Mr. Maverick. To what do I owe the surprise?"

He just wanted to wish her good luck for the banquet, he said. Work was going well. Jessica had brought Lily in for everyone to fawn over, but she was working from home, perhaps forever. "Apparently, they're enjoying parenthood so much, they want to do it again," he told her.

"You sound a little envious. Does Cammie want a lot of children?"

Reese deftly changed the subject, asking about her experience so far in New York. "I'm proud of you. You deserve a broader audience for your art, and this may get your foot in the door. You should visit some of the galleries while you're here, go to the museums."

"I'd love to! Maybe I'll meet someone tonight who's also visiting, and we can check things out together. But either way, I've got a few days. I don't mind going alone—not as much fun alone, but then again, what is?" Andy realized that as she talked, her free hand had slipped between her legs, absentmindedly fingering the short curls there. *What, indeed.*

Reese, ever the journalist, focused on details. "Will the banquet be open seating; will the contestants be together or what?"

Andy frowned. "I have no idea. Hold on." *Odd question.* She found the banquet packet on the bedside table and scanned through several paragraphs. "There's a phone number here to call if you need further information, but I'm good. I don't care where I sit. I'm just looking forward to it." She sighed. "I'm also looking forward to it being *over* if that makes sense."

"Of course, it does. You've been moving toward this one point in time for weeks now. I'm warning you, there may be a bit of a let-down after. I mean, not that you'll be disappointed! I hope you win it *all*! But…" Reese was fumbling for words, not typical for him.

"I understand," Andy said as she laid her head back on the pillow. "Jeffrey was so excited for graduation to get here, and then the next morning, he woke up and didn't have anything to look forward to, at least until school starts. Same kind of thing. He's spending more time with his father, though, so that's good."

Andy chattered on about Humphrey and what was going on there but finally said she needed to go. "I've got a lot of nervous pacing to do. I might head outside for a bit, not sure. Thanks again for calling! That was sweet."

Instead of wasting the entire day in the room, or risking some mishap in the city, Andy decided to let Exagora's money treat her to another new experience—an eye-opening and mind-blowing day at the hotel's exclusive spa. The seaweed wrap was definitely something she would tell the ladies about back home, but it paled in comparison to the massage from Rudolfo.

Nervous when the masseur walked into the room, she was soon put at ease by his firm, practiced touch. There was nothing sexual about the massage, but as he worked on her, Andy imagined what it would be like to have someone who loved her touch her like that. She tried to engage Rudolfo in conversation, but he encouraged her to let her thoughts go. "Listen to the music. Listen to my fingers playing out the tension. Let go of everything." It had been excellent advice.

At six o'clock, Andy rode the elevator down to the ball-room. Her sheath gown was expensive by her standards, but Kristina had assured her that its appeal was timeless. Simple, but elegant. "Like the cars you like. Think of this as an Austin-Healey gown," she'd told her, which had made Andy laugh.

On the elevator, Andy saw her reflection in the mirrored wall and laughed again. The material of the long gown with a plunging back and flattering neckline really *was* the same shade of cobalt blue as Reese's car. No doubt Helen Hamilton would call that a Freudian slip on Andy's part, a sign of her continued thoughts about Reese. Andy regularly met with Helen for counseling now, and she could tell it was having positive results.

As the elevator made its slow, steady descent, Andy fingered her necklace, the one George Sanderson had given her years before. She'd discussed the necklace with Helen and with Kristina, assuring them that she didn't want to wear it to the banquet out of any tenderness toward him. It was an act of pure defiance. She wanted to proclaim that he hadn't ruined her life, that she had risen above it. One day, she would throw the necklace away and be done with him forever. But tonight, the necklace reminded her of how far she had come from the gullible, frightened fourteen year old he had taken advantage of.

When the elevator doors opened, Andy followed signs to the ballroom. Outside the open double doors, she meandered through the many handsome men and elegant women already admiring the contest entries displayed on the walls. When she found her own work, she was delighted to overhear others talking about its creativity and boldness. "I would drive that," one woman commented.

She had told herself, many times in the last few weeks, that she had no chance of winning. As she wandered around viewing the other entries, she decided that she had been correct. Although most of the designs were less innovative than hers, they would be easier to manufacture. In the automobile industry, what mattered was the bottom line. Her car would be too expensive to build, too expensive to purchase. She shrugged, admiring the entry she deemed to be more of a contender, and was startled by a voice behind her.

"Do you like my car?" A swarthy foreign man spoke with a heavy Middle Eastern accent.

"Very much," she said with a smile, extending her hand to shake. "Hey, there. My name is Andy Cummings. And you are?"

The man took her hand and kissed it. "Charmed, Miss Cummings. Shall we look around together?" He offered his arm, which she took shyly.

Chatting easily with the man as they walked up and down the hallway, Andy did not see Reese Maverick looking around the room, a confused expression on his face.

How hard can it be to spot the only bald woman in the room? Reese had arrived in town that morning, checking in with the association for details after speaking with Andy. His two-star hotel was clean and comfortable enough, but he had endured a whirlwind cab ride to get to the Ritz on time. He couldn't ask Andy what she was wearing—that would've spoiled his surprise. But he hadn't counted on it being difficult to find her. The woman he sought stood out in a crowd. To borrow one of her father's phrases, where in the Sam Hill was she?

His eyes zeroed in on a particularly shapely woman just ahead, hanging on the arm of a dashing man who looked to be Middle Eastern. *Aren't you the lucky bastard?* he thought. The woman's stunning figure was encased in yards of shimmering blue; her dark curls shone under the chandeliers. When she turned around, Reese drew in a breath. *Andy?*

Andy's eyes grew wide as they met his. She literally jumped up and down, animating the bodice of her gown in such a way that his eyes almost rolled back in their sockets. He watched as she said something to man she was with before practically running to his side. "Oh my god!" she squealed, giving him an enthusiastic hug. "How are you here? Why?" She looked all around. "Where's Cammie? Is her family part of this?"

"Your hair." *Brilliant opening line, Mav. Just brilliant.*

Andy giggled and grabbed one of his hands to feel the curls. "It grew back, silly. When Mama Wilson's hair started coming back in, I stopped shaving it. I didn't know it would be curly, though! What do you think?"

I think I'm completely, totally in love with you. I think I came all the way to New York to tell you that. "It looks nice!" he said. "Really nice. You look really nice, Andy. And, um, Cammie's not here."

Andy looked at him strangely. "Ooookay. Thank you? Have you seen my car yet?" Without waiting for a reply, she pulled him in the right direction. As she did, Reese glanced back at the Middle Eastern man she'd been with. He raised his eyebrows at Reese, who shrugged and flashed a smile as if to say, *Sorry buddy. Her choice.*

Andy's painting was, as he might have guessed, unlike anyone else's entry. She chattered on about starting with sketches, then colored pencils, but she had gone with bright acrylics for the entry, with framed sketches of the interior motor design hanging beside it. While most of the contestants had merely provided a car design, Andy had filled in an intricate background with people. There was even a driver behind the wheel.

"That's you! This is great!" he said enthusiastically, putting his arm around her as they stood before her work. "I'm so proud of you." He reached into his bag and pulled out his camera. "I want a photo of you; hang on."

Andy posed, a little self-conscious with the crowd milling around, but she noted that others were also taking photos here and there. "So why are you even here? Are y'all in the city visiting Cammie's family? That's so cool you could stop by and see me too. Thank you! You look very handsome, by the way, very sophisticated in that tux."

"I'm staying for the banquet, silly. I wouldn't miss it. Let's go find our seats," he suggested. As they walked, he explained that he had pitched a story for the magazine. "Cars have universal appeal," he said, and following up on her participation would tie this article in with his first. "I have some other things in mind, too."

"Tell me," she said. "I'm here for three more nights, unless I need to stay for some reason. Kristina okayed an extension as long as I'm back for her wedding. Can you believe it? Exagorà House is paying for the whole trip."

A server directed them to the contestants' table, where Reese pulled out Andy's chair for her. "I'm not used to such gentlemanly manners," she whispered to him, but clearly, she enjoyed the treatment. "Do you have to sit at a press table or something? Do you even get to eat?"

Reese laughed softly as he sat down beside her. "I ate in Humphrey, when I was working."

"Good point. Well, we can visit until the others get here."

Reese hung his camera bag on the corner of his seat back. "I'm staying. I'm eating. I am, in fact, your date. Apparently, every contestant was awarded two seats and I barged in on one of yours. I hope you don't mind." He had discreetly confirmed that she hadn't brought anyone along, although he was fairly sure the Middle Eastern man would have found a way to sit there if it hadn't been claimed. *So far, so good. We'll get through the evening, and then I'll tell her how I feel. Tonight, is about her. I've waited this long. I can wait a little longer. If all goes well in that department, this will be a love story for our readers like no other.*

The conversation at this particular table of twelve contestants was pleasant. Andy was pleased to discover that she wasn't the only person there who confessed to feeling nervous, although she was the only woman, apparently, who had entered.

"Darling, I think you have your name cards switched," a

sweet-looking blonde woman helpfully pointed out as salads were placed before them. "That could be a problem for the servers if you and your husband ordered different entrees."

Andy blushed as she picked up her card and looked at it. "No, that's right. I'm Andy, and he's Reese. But we're not married." The others who heard laughed. Everyone else had assumed the cards were mixed up, too.

"Then *you're* the artist, Andy Cummings?" the blonde's companion asked, a rugged redhead with a black suit and bolo tie. "We like your painting very much. Mine's the camouflage truck with a few distinctions." He grinned. "I like to hunt. Can you tell?"

The contestants chatted during the salad course and on through dinner, friendly but also realizing that each one there was hoping to win, and thus, in competition with one another. Only one grand prize winner would be announced. Not every contestant had come to the banquet, but it was Reese's opinion that one of their dinner companions, or someone from one of the other contestants' tables, would leave $5000 richer. Andy told him she favored the Middle Eastern man's entry, delighted when Reese rolled his eyes and made a sarcastic comment. He squeezed Andy's knee under the table and whispered another, "Good luck."

"I'm not going to win," Andy whispered back. "But I needed to try. Maybe meet some people who could help direct me." She winked at him. "Like the Middle Eastern man. He seems nice." When his eyes narrowed in playful response, she shook her head in seriousness, making her curls dance. She took a drink of what Reese knew to be expensive wine and made a little face. "I'd prefer a cold beer, but this is okay. I came for clarity, Reese. Am I a great mechanic who paints a little? Maybe so."

The two continued to eat their entrees, Reese studying her with a frown.

"What? I'm not settling. I just want what Ian calls an 'a-ha moment.' Some focus, some wisdom. I can live with whatever happens, I think. If I need to put all the other ideas and dreams and silliness to rest, I'm ready to do that." She shrugged. "But if there *is* a life outside of Humphrey for me, I'd like to start living it sooner, rather than later. Does that make sense?"

Reese nodded and mumbled an, "Excuse me," as he left the table. *Well, thanks for the encouragement, Reese. I pour out my thoughts and suddenly you need to pee?*

By the time Reese returned, the Middle Eastern man from the hallway had walked over from a nearby table and stood behind Reese's chair, engaged in serious conversation with Andy. They were both contestants, both loved cars, both artists, but she could tell his interest was at a more basic level. She was careful to avoid giving off any encouraging vibes, but she was also flattered. *You never know. Reese has Cammie. Blondie has Camo man. Why shouldn't I have a good time in New York too?*

When Reese approached, he stood beside the artist trying not to look too annoyed, until Andy and he noticed. Reese pointed to the chair. "Excuse me, but that's my seat."

The man apologized, bowed slightly to Andy, and slipped back to his table.

"What was that all about?" he asked with a scowl.

"Just being neighborly, I guess," Andy said, buttering a roll.

Reese looked at her in amazement. "He was not 'just being neighborly'! He was coming on to you. I could tell. He's a man, for heaven's sake. Believe me, I am more—"

Andy smiled at him sadly, mistaking his attitude. "I know; I know. You're more sophisticated than I am. I'm just a girl from the fucking sticks," she said, looking around to make sure no one could overhear. "But you know what? He didn't talk to me like I was from the sticks. Also, he's handsome, has an accent, and seems to think I'm the best thing since sliced bread." She was confused by his tone of voice.

A look of horror crossed Reese's face. "I wasn't going to say that. I *wouldn't* say that."

Andy blushed. Reese had shown up for her big night, whether to write a story or support her, it didn't matter. He was there, and he didn't have to be. "I'm sorry. Helen would say I was projecting, just then. I'm *not* sophisticated; that's obvious. So I expected you to think that too. I expect everyone to think that, but that guy didn't seem to." She popped a big bite of hot bread in her mouth. "Honestly, think about Cammie. Look at the other women here, just at this one table. They're *dripping* with sophistication. I never will," she said around a mouthful of food, "and frankly, I don't want to."

Andy could feel herself move dangerously close to an outburst and she made a conscious effort to take things down a notch. She took a deep breath. "I've made some changes since you left, but I'm still me. Under this, this Cinderella-fucking-ball-gown, I'm still a mechanic from Humphrey." She narrowed her eyes. "So what *were* you going to say?"

An announcement from the front of the room shifted their focus. The program was starting. In all directions, servers removed plates and refilled glasses. There were several speeches with camera flashes popping throughout. Dignitaries in the automotive industry were recognized and applauded. Finally, the moment Andy and the other contestants had been waiting for arrived.

A red velvet curtain rose behind the president of the association, revealing all of the contest entries on easels. It had been a record year, he announced, with most of the contestants returning artists. The winners were announced with great pomp and applause, beginning with five honorable mentions, who went forward to receive $250 each. Third place was announced. Second place. Andy held her breath.

"And the grand prize, $5000 and a contract with a major automobile manufacturer goes to…Nate Whelchel of Freemont, Montana, for his ingenious camouflage truck!"

Nate kissed his wife and walked forward, grinning from ear to ear. He gave a little speech that elicited laughter from the audience, but Andy didn't hear. She had told herself she wouldn't win but realized now that deep down, she'd hoped for at least an honorable mention. She turned to Reese with tears in her eyes. "Well, that's it. I got the answer I was looking for. Looks like I'm a pretty good mechanic after all."

Reese was about to say something as Nate walked back to the table, but out of the corner of his eye, he saw that a server had interrupted the president. Something about the action made Reese stop, tap Andy on the arm, and point back to the podium.

The president unfolded the note and cleared his throat to get everyone's attention. "It seems we have one more award to give this evening. I am pleased to announce that our esteemed panel of judges unanimously felt that one newcomer showed exceptional talent, and they have arranged with several prestigious artists and galleries to offer a year of intensive study to Mister…excuse me…to *Miss* Andy Cummings."

Andy sat for a second in shocked silence as applause filled the ballroom. Reese stood and pulled her chair out for her, leaning down to whisper, "Whatever you do, don't say 'fuck' over the microphone!"

Gliding to the front, Andy climbed the stairs to the stage as an assistant held her painting up for the audience to view. The president handed her a letter from the judges, explaining the details, and asked her to say a few words.

"Thank you so much," Andy said clearly, shaking her head in amazement. "I appreciate it. Really. This changes everything. You have no idea."

An hour after the banquet finally ended, Reese walked Andy to her room. They had talked with many of the audience members, including several of the judges, who offered personal feedback. The car design was impractical, but her presentation had been superior, warranting—in their collective opinion—the extraordinary steps to secure her a residency. Of course, it would be up to her to avail herself of the opportunity, but they hoped she would.

They were alone on the elevator. Andy chattered away while Reese stood a foot away, awkwardly silent. "Hey, you never told me what you were about to say. You said, 'I'm more' and I interrupted you. More what?"

Reese said nothing. "May I see your room? Mine is pretty grim, but it's okay. I'd like to see how the wealthy among us live."

Andy laughed. "I thought you'd been here before with Cammie. Why aren't you staying with her folks? Because it's work?"

The elevator door opened, and Andy pulled her room key from her evening bag. "It's just here," she said, walking to the door. She opened it and gestured him inside. "Isn't it grand? I still can't believe I'm here, and now I can *train* in New York? What a night. And the best part is you were here with me. That means a lot. I appreciate Cammie loosening the chains so you could come." She dangled a card that she pulled from her bag. "From Mr. Amir Wasem, who would like to have dinner with me. Maybe we could double date!"

Reese had walked to the window to admire the view of Central Park. When he turned around, his face was strange. "No, thank you. And will you please stop talking about Cammie? Cammie is no longer part of my life."

Andy joined him at the window with genuine concern in

her eyes. "Oh, Reese. I didn't know! I'm so sorry she—"

"I broke it off with her. When I got home from Humphrey."

"But why? I mean, I'll grant you she's a handful and a half, but—"

Reese was suddenly standing very close, lifting her face for a long and tender kiss that grew more heated by each passing minute. His hands explored her back as she hugged him tightly in disbelief. When he finally released her mouth, he didn't let go, whispering as he kissed the top of her head, her neck, her shoulders, "I love you, Andy Cummings."

Reese picked her up in his arms. "I have dreamed of this moment every day since I left Humphrey, Andy. How could I stay engaged to another woman? You had my heart from the first second I saw you and that crazy bald head and those ridiculous overalls."

Andy arched one eyebrow. "And you were going to say—"

"That *I'm more* aware of your effect on men than you could possibly know. You had Amir Hoozit's attention, all right, and that of every straight man in the room, most of all *mine*. I didn't want to tell you before, though. Tonight, was about you. I'm so proud of you, Andy."

Andy looked down at her chest. Her gown had shifted in his arms, and one breast threatened to pop free of the material. "Uh oh," she whispered and wriggled from his arms, pulling the dress back into place. She could tell that he was disappointed and let him think, for a second, that she was ready for him to leave.

"I guess I'll see you in the morning then," he said.

Instead, Andy backed up to him. "Would you help me with the zipper?" she said quietly. When the zipper was down, she turned to face him and let the gown fall to the floor as she slipped out of her new lace panties. "Stay with me tonight. Please."

16

Reese and Andy

A ndy stepped closer to Reese, reaching for his hands and bringing them around her so he could explore her naked shape as she slipped his arms out of his jacket, unfastened his bow tie and unbuttoned his shirt. Their tongues and mouths savored one another as her hands found her way into his trousers, unfastening here, unzipping there. She had not seen an erect penis up close since that awful day at the lake with George Sanderson, but there was no fear tonight. She was no longer fourteen. And she knew the man before her had nothing on his mind but his love for her, the celebration of the *us* they would become.

Andy glanced over at the bed they were about to share, topped with the plush and pristine duvet. "I-I haven't done this before," she murmured. "I may bleed. Maybe not, but the bed." She'd waited so long for this night, she hated to be thinking of mere practicalities.

Reese raised his eyebrows. It hadn't occurred to him that there hadn't been anyone, ever, who had gotten this close to her. "I've got an idea." Walking into the bathroom, he brought back a towel, then pulled his jacket from where it had fallen and laid it on top. "Just in case. But I'm going to go very, very slow."

"Wait!" Andy cried suddenly.

The hopeful look in Reese's eyes clouded over with longing. "You're not ready. I understand."

"Oh shut the fuck up," she said, punching him in the chest. "Tear this chain off my neck." She held the gold chain up for him to grab. "I don't want it anymore, and I want you to be the one to break it."

Reese frowned, not understanding, but slid one hand between the chain and the back of her neck so it wouldn't dig into her skin, yanking hard with the other and flinging it across the room when the links separated. "Now, are you ready?"

She nodded, biting her lower lip with longing. Reese laid Andy back onto the bed with the jacket under her hips. "May I taste you?"

There was nothing she would deny this man for the rest of her life. She nodded as he knelt on the bed and gently separated her legs. His mouth kissed her inner thighs and licked at the dark curls before his tongue pierced through to the lips they hid. His tongue darted in and out, following every contour thoroughly and gently as her hips began to move in concert. She had become skillful at pleasuring herself with her own hands, but this was absolute bliss. She felt the wave begin to swell.

"Reese?" she said.

He raised his head.

"What do I taste like?"

Reese smiled and crept toward her, kissing her long and hard on the mouth. "Like this," he said hoarsely. "Sweet." He was on his hands and knees over her. She moved her hands along his tightly muscled sides, around to his buttocks, then between his legs spread on either side of her hips. Gently, she traced her fingers down his abdomen and reached for his balls, barely touching them as she watched his face. His eyes were closed as she tickled them softly.

"They're hot," she whispered. "I didn't know they'd be hot."

Reese reached for one of her hands and wrapped her fingers around his cock. "This is hotter."

Andy closed her eyes, afraid she would see the lake in her mind. She didn't. All she felt was passion and desire. She needed this man to be inside her. He was so hard, and she was so soft. She pulled him closer as she spread her legs wide to welcome him. He moved a little closer, until just the head of his penis touched her. She spread her labia and guided him slowly inside. A little more. A little more. It was maddening! Andy grabbed his buttocks and pulled him inside with all her might. For a second, they both held their breaths, their eyes wide.

Andy shook her head and smiled. "I thought it would hurt."

Reese began to move his hips gently. "I've never felt a woman so ready for me to love her."

Andy moved her hips with him, wrapping her legs around him, shifting until the contact was exactly where she needed it to be. Moving as one, they crashed into one another like a waterfall reaching the edge of a cliff and flowing suddenly, mightily to a quiet pool below. As his climax exploded, hers took over, and then slowly, their cries became breaths, their breaths became murmurs, their murmurs became silence.

Reese lifted his weight from her to gaze at her, his eyebrows raised in surprise "Did you?"

She nodded with a grin.

"I didn't think women had orgasms their first time."

Andy caressed his buttocks, feeling his cock harden again inside her when she did. "It wasn't my first orgasm, silly. I figured some things out on my own but this...*you*...are a huge improvement."

"Huge, you say!" Reese laughed, starting his thrusts again. "What the woman wants, the woman gets."

They lay side by side, physically spent at last. "I knew it should be like this, but I didn't think I would ever experience it," Andy murmured with a sigh. She rolled over to face Reese. "You are an amazing man."

Reese turned over and stroked the little curl of hair by her ear. "You are an amazing woman. I have always known that." His hand traced along her hip as he looked down. What he saw made him back away slightly.

"Is something wrong?"

Reese got up and quickly walked into the bathroom. Andy heard water running. Soon, he returned with several steaming washcloths. "Close your eyes and roll over onto your back."

She obeyed. The next sensation she felt was incredibly soothing. Reese gently washed her with the hot cloth. "That feels wonderful."

Without a word, Reese rolled her onto the sheet and continued to tidy her up before removing the towel and jacket that had been beneath her. "There," he said finally. He went back to the bathroom for a second and then lay beside her again. "All done. That, at least, will never be necessary again. You, my dear, are no longer a virgin."

Andy giggled. "*I'll* say. I've been thoroughly made love to *and* had sex *and* been fucked royally tonight. You are a man of great thoroughness, Mr. Maverick."

The next few days were filled with museums, galleries, fine dining and return visits to Bob's Hot Dog Cart in Central Park, a tour of famous sites, and follow-up meetings with contacts the judges had arranged. There were phone calls to the office (Reese) and Humphrey (Andy) explaining what had happened and when they would return to their respective destinations. Their nights were filled with passionate exploration and deep discussions of their future, singular.

He would stay with the magazine for now. She would move to New York, courtesy of the generous grant the judges had arranged, but not until she had time at home to tie up loose ends. She wanted to make sure her father was settled. She wanted to help Jeffrey adjust to his new life as a teacher's aide. "And the wedding!" she exclaimed. "Can you come to Humphrey for Ian and Kristina's wedding?"

"Only if I get to sleep with the bridesmaid."

The weather on Cameron Mountain was perfect. The sky was, as Will announced, "Carolina blue," after the University of North Carolina's trademark school color. The Cummings' house was filled with out-of-town guests, as was Ellen Clark's and Marilda's. Worth and Jessica had sent a gift envelope by way of Layla and Keith, but they'd decided not to make the trip with newborn Lily.

"A cruise!" Kristina said, reading the card they sent. "I've never been on a cruise, have you? And we can go whenever we want—the vouchers are good for a year."

Ian shook his head and took her in his arms. "They could send us to the South Pole, for all I care. This time tomorrow, we will be Mr. and Mrs. Ian Cameron."

Pete and Marilda's gift was paying for a local trio to provide music. Chip and Ellen had paid for the catering, courtesy of Francine's Diner, closed for the week in preparation. And Francine and her new beau—Jeff Wilson, Sr.—had evidently enjoyed working together on the pans and trays of what she called "vittles" to spread out on rented tables.

Finally, the time had come. Ellen Clark, a notary public, had applied for a special one-day provision in order to marry the couple at their request. She stood now on the front porch of the cabin, surveying the well-wishers sitting in chairs in the clearing. Family, friends, teachers, former pupils, representatives from Ian's mother's tribe, all sat in happy anticipation.

Ian stood to her left, with Will and Chip beside him as they listened to the pleasant sound of fiddle, guitar, and string bass playing in the background. At the proper time, Angela walked slowly between the two sections of guests, throwing wildflowers for a little path to follow. Behind her, Andy carried a bouquet of wildflowers she had helped Kristina gather from the mountain the day before. She found Reese in the group and blew him a kiss.

Layla followed, smiling at her husband Keith, Jessica's mother Carol and Keith's father Chet, who were sitting, holding hands, and then at Ian. Being around him these past few days, she had been charmed by him herself. Her heart was full of happiness for her little sister and this new addition to their family.

When the wedding party was in place, the trio began a new song to announce the arrival of the bride. Everyone stood as Kristina walked around from the kitchen door of the cabin— off limits to Ian all day—past the musicians, past the chairs, and down the flower-strewn ribbon of grass leading to Ian, and to her new life as his wife.

As Kristina walked, she thought back over the last year. She had arrived in Poplar Gap, a woman in the process of healing, but today, she felt her heart would burst with joy. It had taken tears, counseling, getting snowed-in and spanked, being bitchy, and making lifelong friends, but she felt she had finally come home for good.

The music stopped as Kristina took her place beside Ian.

"Dearly beloved," Ellen Clark's strong voice carried into the clearing, "we are gathered together here in the sign of God—and in the face of this company—to join together this man and this woman in holy matrimony, which is commended to be honorable among all men; and therefore—is not by any—to be entered into unadvisedly or lightly—but reverently, discreetly, advisedly and solemnly. Into this holy estate, these two persons present now come to be joined. If any person can show just cause why they may not be joined together—let them speak now or forever hold their peace."

"I need to pee. Can't hold it," Angela's voice piped up.

Layla bent down to whisper to her as a wave of soft laughter moved through the guests. Ellen Clark looked at the flower girl with her best "principal" face and Angela nodded solemnly.

Ellen continued. "Marriage is the union of husband and wife in heart, body and mind. It is intended for their mutual joy—and for the help and comfort given one another in prosperity and adversity. But more importantly—it is a means through which a stable and loving environment may be attained. We are here today to witness the joining in marriage of Ian Cameron and Kristina Edwards. This occasion marks the celebration of love and commitment with which this man and this woman begin their life together. Before the exchanging of rings and vows, I will now read a traditional Cherokee blessing. Ian, this was read to your parents at their marriage, and I know they are watching over you today."

God in heaven above, please protect the ones we love. We honor all you created as we pledge our hearts and lives together. We honor Mother Earth and ask for our marriage to be abundant and grow stronger through the seasons. We honor fire and ask that our union be warm and glowing with love in our hearts. We honor wind and ask that we sail through life safe and calm as in our fathers' arms. We honor water to clean and soothe our relationship—that it may never thirst for love. With all the forces of the universe you created, we pray for harmony as we grow forever young together. Amen.

"Ian, do you take this woman to be your wife, to live together in holy matrimony, to love her, to honor her, to comfort her, and to stay with her in sickness and in health, forsaking all others, for as long as you both shall live?"

Ian's voice was strong and steady. "I do."

"Kristina—my precious Kristina," Ellen continued, her voice breaking with emotion, but quickly back under her control, "do you take this man to be your husband, to live together in holy matrimony, to love him, to honor him, to comfort him, and to stay with him in sickness and in health, forsaking all others, for as long as you both shall live?"

Kristina beamed at Ian. "I do."

Will handed Ian the simple silver ring his mother had worn too briefly. Layla handed Kristina their father's wedding band.

Ian looked out at the guests. "This ring was a symbol of my father's love for my mother. It is now a symbol of my never-ending love for Kristina."

Kristina smiled at them as she held her gift to Ian high. "This ring was a symbol of our mother's love for our father. It is now a symbol of my never-ending love for Ian."

They turned back to face Ellen, who had tears streaming down her face. "By virtue of the authority vested in me under the laws of the State of North Carolina, I now pronounce you husband and wife." She paused while everyone waited. And waited. Ellen looked at Kristina, who opened her eyes wide and pursed her lips for a hint.

"Oh!" Ellen's deep laugh rang through the tree. "I almost forgot the best part. Ian, you may now kiss your bride!"

The trio struck up a lively tune as well-wishers, coworkers, family and friends gathered around the newly married couple and separated into little clumps of conversation. Jeff and Francine, along with Jeffrey and staff from the diner, began pulling out platters of steaming food from the back of the van parked to one side of the yard.

Children played, Blue barked happily with the music, couples danced, and everyone feasted until they couldn't eat another bite.

As twilight descended on Cameron Mountain and the first stars appeared overhead, Reese and Andy held each other close as a slow ballad played. In a month or so, she would leave the mountains, committed to the artist-in-residence program for at least nine months. In the morning, Reese would fly back to the city, where he would work hard, save money, and count the days until they could share a weekend again.

"Andy," he said now.

Andy lifted her head from where it rested on his chest as they danced. "Yes?"

"I'd feel a whole lot better about leaving tomorrow if you'd just do one thing for me."

"What's that?" Andy laid her head back down as their feet kept time to the music.

Reese stopped dancing. Andy stopped dancing. Other guests, sensing that something was about to happen, watched as Reese dropped to one knee and pulled something that caught the starlight from his shirt pocket. He held it up and looked around, laughing softly at being the center of attention.

Clearing his throat, his voice rose so that everyone could hear. "Andy Cummings, however long it takes to make it happen, will you marry me?"

Epilogue

A trim, dark-haired young man patiently explained the paintings currently featured at his exclusive Manhattan gallery to a woman whose knowledge of art was scant at best. Although elegantly coiffured and attired, she seemed to be more interested in what would look best over her new sofa in the new living room of her new home on Long Island than what constituted a true work of art.

"I just don't know," she fretted as the tiny dog she carried in her purse stuck its head out and yipped. "Ritzy! I'm almost done, and then Mummy will take you for a ride." She smiled at the young man. "I named him for the Ritz-Carlton, where I met my husband." She winked. "My latest husband, that is. Mummy never needed babies, did she, Ritzy? You're my baby, aren't you?"

The young man refrained from comment as the woman strolled aimlessly around the gallery, trying to decide. "I think I'll take this one," she said finally, choosing the largest and most expensive painting on display. "Yes, this will just have to do, I suppose. I'll have my designer make accent pillows in silk to match the vibrant blue. Yes, that will tie things together nicely. Such a happy shade."

The young man smiled. "An excellent choice, ma'am. And you're right. It *is* a happy shade, the same shade of blue as my father's vintage Austin-Healey, as a matter of fact. The same shade, they tell me, as the gown my mother wore one very special night." He went to his desk to begin the necessary paperwork for the sale.

"An Austin-Healey!" the woman exclaimed. "Humph. I used to know a man who had one of those, and I believe his was that same color. What a fascinating coincidence. He was completely unsuitable for *me*, but he certainly tried his best to woo me." She pulled out her checkbook. "To whom shall I write the check? To the gallery, or to you or—"

"To the artist herself, ma'am. Make it out to Andrea Maverick." His eyes twinkled with pride. "My mother."

The End

Emily Sharpe

Emily Sharpe is the pen name for a writer, editor and illustrator in south Florida. A former newspaper columnist, she loves to travel and perform in community theater. Mother of four and grandmother of five, Emily substitute teaches, sings, volunteers in the community and attends a raucous group of writers once a month called "Use Your Words." She heartily believes in love and finding one's joy – and she hopes you enjoy this story of romance. Readers may contact her by e-mail: emilysharpebooks@gmail.com.

Don't miss these exciting titles by Emily Sharpe and Blushing Books!

Dear Editor series
Dear Editor
The Stonemason and the Lady
Mating Season
Running Hot

Audible Books
Dear Editor

Blushing Books

Blushing Books is one of the oldest eBook publishers on the web. We've been running websites that publish spanking and BDSM related romance and erotica since 1999, and we have been selling eBooks since 2003. We hope you'll check out our hundreds of offerings at http://www.blushingbooks.com.

Blushing Books Newsletter

Please join the Blushing Books newsletter
to receive updates & special promotional offers.
You can also join by using your mobile phone:
Just text BLUSHING to 22828.